Love
Most Certain

LOVE LETTERS FROM ELLIS CREEK

Cheryl ~
Enjoy your glimpse into the lives of Genevieve and Oliver!
Blessings,
Penny Zeller ~
Psalm 19:14

Love Most Certain

LOVE LETTERS FROM ELLIS CREEK

3

PENNY ZELLER

ALSO BY PENNY ZELLER

Maplebrook Publishing

Standalone Books
Love in Disguise
Love in the Headlines
Freedom's Flight

Wyoming Sunrise
Love's New Beginnings
Forgotten Memories
Dreams of the Heart
When Love Comes
Love's Promise

Love Letters from Ellis Creek
Love from Afar
Love Unforeseen
Love Most Certain

Chokecherry Heights
Henry and Evaline (Prequel)
Love Under Construction

Horizon Series
Over the Horizon
Dreams on the Horizon
Beyond the Horizon

Whitaker House Publishing

Montana Skies
McKenzie
Kaydie
Hailee

Barbour Publishing

Love from Afar
*(The Secret Admirer
Romance Collection)*

Freedom's Flight
*(The Underground Railroad
Brides Collection)*

Beacon Hill Press
(Nonfiction)

77 Ways Your Family Can
Make a Difference

Dedicated to my readers.

And whatsoever ye do, do it heartily,
as to the Lord, and not unto men.
Colossians 3:23

Chapter One

GENEVIEVE AMSEL SETTLED INTO her new room at Mrs. Vannostrand's boarding house. "I know I've mentioned it at least a dozen times, but I'm ecstatic you decided to move to Ellis Creek," her closest friend, Tillie Fairbanks, said.

A niggle of doubt weaved its way through Genevieve's heart, but she dismissed it. Living in Ellis Creek was preferable to residing in Fentonville after Irving decided to sever their engagement so close to the wedding date. Expectation flickered in Tillie's eyes and she edged closer, likely awaiting Genevieve's confirmation that moving to Ellis Creek *had* been a grand idea.

Genevieve wouldn't allow her concerns to damper Tillie's enthusiasm. "I'm ecstatic to be here." It was an honest statement for the most part. Tillie's parents, Mr. and Mrs. Waller, had opened their home to her and she'd stayed with them until a room at Mrs. Vannostrand's boarding house became available. Moving to the boarding house cemented Genevieve's decision to begin anew.

Tillie placed a hand on Genevieve's arm. "I've been praying for the Lord to heal your broken heart."

"Thank you, Tillie. I know He will in time. I never imagined Irving would do such a thing. And Aunt Blanche is beside herself with concern that I will become a spinster and the high society folks of Fentonville will look down upon her and Uncle Richard for my failed engagement."

"Oh, dear. It's just as well that you moved here then." Tillie paused. "I wasn't going to say as much while you and Irving were courting, but I honestly don't believe he would have made a suitable husband."

At one time in the not-too-distant past, Genevieve believed with all her being that Irving was the one God had chosen for her. That they would live happily in Fentonville and would someday have a large family—a desire of Genevieve's since she was an only child and secretly envied those with siblings. She sighed. "I never would have agreed with you on that matter until Irving

Shewbridge paid a visit that day and told me he didn't believe we should marry."

It was almost as if it occurred yesterday, so fresh were the wounds. The arrogant and seemingly uncompassionate manner in which he relayed the information to her led Genevieve to believe he'd never really loved her.

And did you ever really love him? Genevieve shoved the thought aside. Yes, she had loved him. Hadn't she?

"I know your aunt and uncle weren't thrilled at the prospect of you moving to Ellis Creek, but I hope it's been a pleasant change for you."

"Indeed it has." Genevieve was relieved to have found friends who accepted her and welcomed her into their lives. Friends like Tillie, Lula Plessner, and Mollie Reuscher.

After Tillie left, Genevieve bustled about the small room, unpacking her belongings. The room boasted a bureau with room on top for her Bible, hairbrush, a book she'd borrowed from Tillie, an oval ornate mirror, and the portrait of her parents, whom she missed every day. She lifted the latter and held it to her heart. What would they have thought about her decision to leave Fentonville and carve a new life for herself in Ellis Creek? Would they have desired for Genevieve to stay with her wealthy aunt and uncle in a life so opposite of the one in which she was raised? Or would they have been proud of her for taking a teaching job in a new town? She propped up the precious photo against the wall and organized the remainder of her belongings.

3

The bed boasted a colorful yellow-and-red quilt and the bowl and pitcher stood on a nearby faded tea cart. A striped rug between the bed and the bureau and a painting hanging above the bed completed the humble room's furnishings.

Genevieve opened the yellow curtains. In the vast yard below, children—most of them her pupils at the school where she now taught—played a game of tag. From her window, she could see the road leading into town, the barber shop, and just beyond that, the edge of Lula's house. The sunny day beckoned her with the promise of new beginnings.

Yes, living in Ellis Creek was just the remedy for a broken heart.

Oliver Bessell peered out the post office window. Dark clouds lingered in the sky, a contrast from the recent sunny weather. Last night it rained, and Mr. Hodgeson asserted at the breakfast table that more rain was to come based on the ache in his elbow.

Oliver returned to the counter and finished sorting the mail when an elderly woman with a bowed back and gray hair tottered into the post office with her cane. "Good afternoon, Mrs. Crabtree," he said.

"It is most certainly *not* a good afternoon, Mr. Bessell. Every day I have more and more ailments, and today my rheumatism is acting up something fierce. It's cloudy rather than sunny outside, the street is muddy from last night's rain, and as such, a careless passerby drove his wagon right through a mud puddle and splashed me with dirty water." She paused and exhaled an exaggerated breath. "The mercantile is plumb out of brown thread, Mrs. Vannostrand is serving ham and pea soup for supper, which is my least favorite meal, and you're here in charge of the post office instead of Mr. Norman."

Oliver gaped at Mrs. Crabtree, no reply coming to mind. He knew of a few townsfolk who failed to hide their irritation that he replaced Mr. Norman, but none had been so bold as to outrightly express their feelings about the matter. "I…"

"Pshaw." She pointed a gnarled finger at him. "And did you know that Mr. Norman never would have allowed the floor to collect any dust? He was forever sweeping it and keeping it neat and tidy. Yet look at it now." Mrs. Crabtree gestured toward the floor where mud, tracked in from previous customers, had yet to be swept. "And the piles of paper and letters on the counter are unacceptable. Mr. Norman never would have allowed that."

Oliver attempted to avoid taking Mrs. Crabtree's criticism to heart as he perused his work area. The pile of letters would soon be remedied when he distributed the mail into the appropriate mail slots. The floor *did* collect dust on any given day and especially today with the abundance of mud. The counter could use a good cleaning, and the stamp and money drawers could be arranged better.

Inwardly he sighed. The morning's busyness had precluded him from properly tending to other less-pressing duties. That and he *did* struggle at times with being disorganized—always had. He even commonly misplaced his spectacles, which he used only for reading.

But in all fairness, he was still learning this position and as time wore on, he would improve. He endeavored to do his best and to do all things "heartily, as to the Lord" as the verse in Colossians stated. Oliver pondered his response to Mrs. Crabtree, who was still muttering about his shortcomings. Finally, when she took a breath, he interjected, "Mrs. Crabtree, I'm sorry you're having a bad day..."

"Not bad, dreadful. Positively dreadful. Wretched and abysmal."

"Mrs. Crabtree, is there something I can do to help you? Have you spoken to the doctor about your rheumatism?"

"My rheumatism is none of your concern. Now, I need to buy a stamp." She placed the coin on the counter and glared at him, unblinking, through round spectacles.

He exchanged the coin for a stamp. "Anything else, ma'am?"

Mrs. Crabtree regarded him for a moment. She pursed her lips, accentuating years of wrinkles around her mouth. "No, nothing more. But do tell Mr. Norman he is welcome back posthaste." She shuffled out of the post office without so much as a backward glance in his direction.

When Oliver received the letter offering him the position in Ellis Creek, he couldn't wait to undertake his new role, even if it meant moving away from his family. But not everyone accepted him as the new postmaster. So far he'd heard of about five of the town's residents who'd begged, pleaded, and even attempted to bribe the popular Mr. Norman to return to his job.

Becoming the new postmaster in Ellis Creek was not for the faint of heart. Oliver pondered many times over if he should relinquish his position and return to Bozeman. Who knew overseeing the mail could be so hazardous to one's self-confidence?

Yet he'd made numerous friends in his new town. Gideon, Will, Jed, Gabe, and several others. He enjoyed and learned much from Reverend Harr's teaching and appreciated the friendliness of the other churchgoers. And most of his fellow residents at the boarding house were amiable folks.

Ma and Pa had encouraged him to proceed with accepting the position, especially since Oliver had long been fascinated with mail delivery. And as one who rarely gave up, he would continue to pray for God's guidance in effectively performing his new role.

Chapter Two

THAT SUNDAY, GENEVIEVE SETTLED into the chair in her room at the boarding house and brushed her long blonde hair, removing any tangles before winding it into a Newport knot. Placing her tortoiseshell combs on each side, she then pinched her cheeks to introduce some color as Aunt Blanche insisted she do. "You're far too pale," her aunt admonished on more than one occasion.

Genevieve opened the top bureau drawer and reached for her earrings, a lovely pair she'd received as a go-ing-away gift from her former pupils in Fentonville. Just as she was about to close the drawer, her gaze fell upon the tintype of Irving Shewbridge. She withdrew it, holding it in the palm of her hand as Irving's likeness stared back at her.

Why she kept the tintype, she had no idea, for it only served as a reminder of her broken heart. While she appreciated being invited to the wedding of two acquaintances yesterday, it *had* been difficult.

There had been a time in the not-too-distant past when she longed for the future she believed would be shared with Irving. After all, hadn't Aunt Blanche indicated he was the perfect addition to their family? Irving was intelligent, wealthy, a banker, and dapper. He attended church and got along well with Uncle Richard. And truth be told, marrying him would free her from residing with her overbearing relatives. She would never want for anything as Aunt Blanche pointedly told her numerous times. Genevieve never cared about wealth. Having never experienced such a lifestyle until she resided with her aunt and uncle, she'd not grown accustomed to it.

Fair complected with brown eyes, white-blond hair, and a perfectly groomed mustache, Irving was a handsome man. He was tall, thin, and well-dressed. And he had no shortage of confidence.

And when Irving asked Genevieve to court him, she thought she might have been dreaming, for who would ask an orphan—who thought herself on the plain side—for her hand in courtship? Looking back, she suspected Uncle Richard may have had a role in Irving's decision.

All was well until Irving decided to break their engagement just weeks before their nuptials. So why then keep the tintype? There was no need to save this reminder of the man who'd broken her heart. She knew the day Irving informed her of his decision that she would never fall in love again, no matter what marital prospects came her way. The heartbreak wasn't worth it.

Thankfully, Tillie promised to pray for her and then invited Genevieve to Ellis Creek and encouraged her to apply for the second teaching position at the school. After Tillie married Will, Genevieve took on the role as the primary teacher.

Ellis Creek had become her home. She quickly made friends with Tillie's family, Lula, Mollie, and several others, and now she couldn't imagine residing anywhere else.

The sound of the breakfast bell pulled Genevieve from her thoughts. She would discard Irving's tintype later. But for now, she returned it to the bureau drawer.

The aroma of bacon and eggs floated on the air and Genevieve took her seat at the table. Mrs. Vannostrand—a widow, who with her young son, Adam, ran the boarding house—had also become a friend. Genevieve scanned the other faces of those at the table. Mrs. Crabtree, a woman who fittingly lived up to her name as she was always cantankerous, sat beside Adam. Mr. and Mrs. Hodgeson, a senescent couple who'd been married forever according to Mrs. Hodgeson, sat next to Genevieve. And across the table sat the new postmaster, Oliver Bessell. A man of about Genevieve's age, he seemed a pleasant sort with his courteous chatter and willingness to help around the boarding house when needed.

Mr. Hodgeson blessed the meal and Genevieve partook in conversation with several of the residents. Mrs. Hodgeson shared about her latest quilt. Mrs. Crabtree complained that her food was cold. Adam talked of his insect collection, and Mr. Bessell discussed cattle prices with Mr. Hodgeson.

When they finished eating, the residents walked as a group to the church. Adam zipped around chasing a butterfly while talking nonstop with his mother. Mrs. Hodgeson linked her hand through the crook of Mr. Hodgeson's elbow. Mrs. Crabtree complained that it was far too hot to be walking, and Mr. Bessell whistled a pleasant tune.

An eclectic group if there ever was one.

Reverend Harr greeted Genevieve as she entered the crowded church. She peered around, noting that everyone, as they did each Sunday, had a place to sit. In her aunt and uncle's church in Fentonville, families clustered together and shared a pew. It was the same in Ellis Creek.

Except that Genevieve didn't have any family here.

If Genevieve asked, she knew Tillie would invite her to sit with her family on their overfull pew or that Lula would huddle together with her large family in an effort to create a meager space on their pew. Or even Mollie with her parents and aunts and uncles would welcome her to sit with them. But Genevieve didn't want to intrude. So instead, she searched for a spot for those who didn't have families.

In the third-to-the-last pew on the right-hand side sat Mrs. Vannostrand, Adam, Mr. and Mrs. Hodgeson, and two unfamiliar people. In the pew directly behind them sat Mr. Bellinger, Mrs. Crabtree, Mr. Norman, and Widow Jones. Genevieve took a seat next to Widow Jones.

The woman greeted her warmly. "Hello, dear."

"Hello, Widow Jones."

"Hopefully there aren't going to be more people in our pew because it's becoming quite cramped," lamented Mrs. Crabtree.

Mr. Norman, a seemingly affable fellow, chuckled. "We still have room for at least one more, Mrs. Crabtree."

Mrs. Crabtree, a permanent scowl on her face, said nothing but wrung her gnarled fingers before folding her arms across her chest.

Widow Jones and Mr. Norman carried on a conversation, Mr. Bellinger bobbed his head as if he were about to fall asleep, and Mrs. Crabtree glowered.

More congregants filed into the small church, most greeting each other warmly before taking their seats. Genevieve observed the ongoings around her and hoped that one day she would consider Ellis Creek her permanent home.

"Do you mind if I sit here?" a voice asked. She looked up to see Mr. Bessell standing at the edge of the pew.

"That would be fine." She scooted over toward Widow Jones so as to provide ample space for the postmaster.

He grinned at her and took his seat. "Thank you. It's always a little nerve-wracking arriving on Sunday not knowing exactly where to sit."

Genevieve concurred. She offered a pleasant smile. "Indeed."

"I suppose it's due to the fact that I don't care much for sitting alone and that I come from a large family and never had to worry where I sat in church."

"Do you like Ellis Creek?"

"I'm still settling in and attempting to find my way, but so far most of the people have been very welcoming."

"I agree. Ellis Creek has a smaller population than Fentonville, but from what Tillie said, the town has grown significantly due to the new mill."

Mr. Bessell nodded. "Yes, that's what I've heard as well."

Reverend Harr took his place behind the pulpit. After announcements and the collection of the tithe, the congregation rose to sing several hymns. Genevieve noticed immediately that Mr. Bessell knew most of the hymns from memory.

"Today's sermon is on how God is our comfort," said the reverend after the parishioners had concluded their singing. "We'll look at several verses today, but let's start with Second Corinthians 1:3-4."

Genevieve quickly located the passage as the reverend read aloud, "*'Blessed be God, even the Father of our Lord Jesus Christ, the Father of mercies, and the God of all comfort; Who comforteth us in all our tribulation, that we may be able to comfort them which are in any trouble, by the comfort wherewith we ourselves are comforted of God.'*"

She listened as he spoke. "The Lord is our comforter. He cares deeply about whatever we are experiencing, whether a small problem or an overwhelming trial."

When her parents died, when she had to go live with an aunt and uncle she'd previously met only once, and when Irving broke her heart, God had been there through those times. Genevieve thanked the Lord for His providence and prayed again for peace and guidance as she continued to embark on her new life in Ellis Creek.

When the service ended, she stood. "Have a good day, Mr. Bessell."

"Please, call me Oliver."

"And you may call me Genevieve."

"Are you staying for the after-service potluck?" Oliver asked, allowing her to step ahead of him into the aisle.

Genevieve appreciated the potlucks held by the church twice a month. "I am."

He sidled alongside her as if they'd long been friends. "So am I. Of course, I never pass up the chance to enjoy some of Widow Jones's rhubarb pie."

They emerged from the church into the sunny day, quite opposite of the recent rainy weather. Genevieve closed her eyes and tilted her face toward the sky for the briefest of moments.

Theodora, Lula's daughter, bounded toward them. "Miss Amsel, Mr. Bessell, Ma wants to know if you'd like to join them over there." She pointed to a place beneath the tree where several people had gathered.

Moments later, Genevieve sat beneath the tree chatting with Tillie, Lula, Mollie, and Meredith. They discussed a variety of topics from sewing, gardening, and children to the upcoming Ellis Creek festivities. But Mollie mostly talked about her friend, Gideon. The menfolk clustered into a circle just to the right, their plates heaping with food, as they conversed about cattle prices, fishing, and horses.

And as Genevieve sat with her new friends, she felt the peace she'd prayed for regarding her move to Ellis Creek.

This *was* her home.

Chapter Three

THE FOLLOWING WEEK, GENEVIEVE was busy preparing her lesson plans for the next day when Adam Vannostrand dashed through the school doorway. "Miss Amsel! Miss Amsel!"

"What is it, Adam?"

"Mr. Bessell says you have a letter at the post office."

Genevieve marveled how Adam could still be so energetic after morning chores, a full day of school, and playing baseball with his friends after school. "Thank you. I am just finishing here and will retrieve it posthaste."

She surmised the letter would be from Aunt Blanche. Hopefully all was well. When Genevieve lived in Fentonville and Tillie would write, she was ecstatic to receive correspondence. However, Aunt Blanche's letters were most often dismal and bland compared to Tillie's. Genevieve cleared her desk in preparation for tomorrow and shut the door behind her. She crossed the street and continued on her way to the post office.

"Hello, Oliver," she greeted.

"Adam must have delivered my message. Here's your letter." Oliver placed an envelope on the counter.

Aunt Blanche's precise and overly-slanted handwriting indicated another lackluster letter. Perhaps she would step outside and sit on the bench on the boardwalk and peruse her aunt's missive.

"How was your day?" Oliver asked, the warmth of his smile reflected in his voice.

She appreciated his consideration. "Busy and eventful. We held class near the creek today and focused on our history lessons. Of course, that swiftly turned to talk of fish and who'd caught the biggest fish. The size of the fish grew with each story." Genevieve laughed as she recalled each pupil's attempt to best the others with their "fish story". "After our arithmetic lesson, we paused for lunch and recess. One of the young scholars wagered he could catch a fish with his bare hands. A contest ensued. Needless to say, within minutes, a fish was flung toward the shore. I daresay the Smith family will be enjoying the catch for supper tonight."

Oliver chuckled, his amusement contagious, and Genevieve laughed along with him as if she'd known him for years instead of weeks.

They exchanged further pleasantries before Genevieve waved goodbye and stepped out onto the mostly empty boardwalk. Few passersby congregated on Main Street at the moment, and she took a seat on the weathered bench. Genevieve lifted the envelope's seal and removed a sheet of Aunt Blanche's customary pale-yellow stationery.

Dear Genevieve,

I trust you are well. Yesterday we received word that Irving has proposed to Wanda Massman. Such wonderful news! Wanda has already chosen her dress from Kunkel's Millinery. It is an exquisite silk gown with plentiful lace and a long train. Wanda is a lovely girl and she and Irving are so in love.

It's a shame you and Irving couldn't marry as your Uncle Richard would have liked to have him as a relative. But we are thrilled for the Massman family.

Do write and tell us how you fare.

Sincerely,

Aunt Blanche

Genevieve swallowed the lump in her throat. Aunt Blanche had always lacked tact. And most of the time, it was over trivial matters. But the news of Irving preparing to marry Wanda so soon after breaking their engagement was difficult to comprehend. Her eyes stung and her shoulders shook. Both her aunt and uncle alluded to the fact they believed the canceled engagement was Genevieve's fault. A tear fell onto the letter, smearing the words.

Her hands shook as she tucked it back into the envelope. It was one thing to not be marrying the man she thought she would wed. It was quite another to read about Aunt Blanche rejoicing that Irving was marrying someone else. Now Genevieve had absolutely no regrets for discarding Irving's tintype last night.

She attempted to bite back the steady flow of tears and slowly trudged down the boardwalk toward home. Hopefully she would be able to dash up the stairs before anyone saw her. Some time in her room alone was just what she needed.

Or was it?

Perhaps Tillie was home and had finished tutoring her last pupil. Some time with her best friend might be more of what she needed than solitary moments basking in her melancholy.

Genevieve pivoted in the opposite direction toward Tillie's house. She entered First Street and followed the road to the third house on the right, an endearing white-washed cottage with a tiny square porch. *Please, Lord, let Tillie be home.*

Tillie opened the door upon Genevieve's first knock. "Genevieve! What an utter delight to see you. I just finished with my last pupil. Do come in." She stepped aside and ushered Genevieve into the tastefully-decorated parlor to the right.

It took her best friend only a moment to realize Genevieve's dolefulness.

"Genevieve? Is everything all right?"

Tillie's concern was all that was needed for the flood of tears to emerge. Without so much as a word, Tillie embraced her and patted her gently on the back.

After several minutes, Tillie took a step back and in an expedient motion, led Genevieve to the sofa, handed her a handkerchief, and proceeded to pour two glasses of lemonade. She took a seat next to her and patted her arm. "How can I help?"

That was Tillie, always helpful and always willing to lend encouragement. Genevieve removed Aunt Blanche's letter and handed it to her friend.

"But, goodness." Tillie read the letter and placed it on the sofa. "I don't know your aunt, but she could use some assistance in diplomacy."

"She's always been that way, and truth be told, she and Uncle Richard believed it was me who canceled our engagement. Irving never could do any wrong in my uncle's eyes, especially since Uncle Richard has been friends with Irving's father since they were youngsters."

Tillie's brow furrowed. "Well, be that as it may, you have my deepest condolences regarding the letter. Not only do you have the grief of your wedding being canceled and the entire town knowing about it, but you also had to contend with that detestable scoundrel marrying so soon after your broken engagement."

"A matter of months, really."

"Irving did not deserve someone like you, Genevieve."

Tillie had mentioned as much before, but to hear her say it again was of great comfort. "It is one thing to know that the wedding I'd dreamed of for months was not to become a reality. It's another that Irving so hastily found someone else. And Wanda Massman is *not* a lovely girl." The tears fell again as Genevieve recalled how hateful and spiteful Wanda was to those beneath her station and how she'd mocked Genevieve for being an orphan.

"Then she and Irving will make the perfect pair."

Tillie's words caused a slight giggle to rise in Genevieve's throat amidst the pain. "Thank you, Tillie, for being here for me. For being the best friend a girl could have."

Tillie gave her another hug. "You are so welcome and I'm grateful for your friendship as well. Let me pray for you. Dear Heavenly Father, we know You are close to the brokenhearted and that You care deeply for us and the things that grieve us. Bring peace and comfort to Genevieve and heal her broken heart. In Jesus' Name, Amen." She rose. "Would you care for some jawbreakers? Lula says they are the cure for just about anything that ails us."

"That sounds delightful. Yes, please."

Tillie returned with a bag of jawbreakers and handed Genevieve several. She again took a seat on the sofa.

"This is why I shall never court someone again. I would be beside myself if what happened with Irving occurred a second time."

Tillie popped a jawbreaker into her mouth. "I know what that ghastly Irving did was despicable and even worse now that he is marrying the unlovely, hateful, and spiteful Wanda. Not to mention Aunt Blanche's letter indicating her excitement regarding the whole affair. But God *will* heal your broken heart." She paused. "And not every man is like Irving. Look at Will or Jed or Gideon. They are nothing like him. Nor is Oliver."

"We don't know Oliver well. He just moved here."

"True, but Will, whom I would say is a superb judge of character, says Oliver is a forthright, honest, and upstanding young man. You know him from the boarding house and you mentioned the other day that the two of you have become friends. Surely you see some of those qualities."

Genevieve considered Tillie's words. "Yes, we are friends, albeit new ones, and yes, I do see those qualities in him. He's also thoughtful and has a pleasing disposition from what I've seen."

"Confirmation then that not all men are like Irving. My pa, Mr. Kleeman, the reverend, Mr. Norman, Mr. Reuscher...they are all kind men. Irving did not deserve you and pray tell, what kind of life would you have had being married to him? Arrogant, selfish, and pompous are words that come to mind regarding his character."

"Now that you mention it, Irving is those things. He only cared about himself."

Tillie nodded. "Yes, and as your best friend, I am honor bound to tell you the honest and bona fide truth about repugnant and loathsome individuals."

In spite of her despondency, Genevieve giggled. "Tillie, you and your descriptive words."

"Am I not correct?"

"You are correct. And whatever would I do without you?"

"And, Genevieve, someday, if it is the Lord's will, you *will* fall in love again with a man deserving of your love. And if marriage is not a door God wishes for you to walk through, He has another more perfect plan for your life."

Tillie's words resonated. Indeed, not all men were like Irving. But she resolved to keep her promise to herself to never again give her heart to another.

Chapter Four

WEDNESDAY MORNING, OLIVER FINISHED sweeping the floor as Tillie and Lula moseyed through the door. Lula carried her youngest in her arms, a chubby baby who favored his pa.

"Good morning, Oliver," said Tillie. "I need to purchase a stamp."

He debated whether or not to tell Tillie and Lula about his concerns regarding Genevieve. Yesterday when she'd received the letter, she proceeded to sit on the bench outside the post office. From the angle in which he'd stood, Oliver could see her clearly although her back was to him. Her shoulders quaking and the way she dabbed at her eyes as she stood to leave clearly indicated the letter contained bad news.

Had someone in her family passed? Oliver knew she was from Fentonville and Widow Jones mentioned she formerly resided with her aunt and uncle. He'd heard from a couple of different townsfolk something about a broken engagement and Will said the way he and Tillie became reacquainted was through a letter-writing campaign organized by Genevieve and Tillie.

But that was all he knew about the delicate and soft-spoken woman who had recently become his friend.

Oliver also knew that one of the main jobs for the postmaster was to stay abreast of the happenings in the town in which he worked. However, Oliver wished to be just the opposite of Bozeman's postmaster, Mr. Barbuto, who fondly shared gossip about the townsfolk. He weighed his options, prayed, then weighed his options again.

"Oliver?" Tillie asked.

He returned his focus to Tillie and Lula. "I noticed Genevieve was quite distraught yesterday," he said, his voice sounding far too formal in his own ears. His sisters would josh him for sure. Perhaps he ought to have added a British accent.

Some unreadable, albeit suspicious, glance passed between the two women before Tillie spoke. "We've actually been worried about Genevieve."

"Oh?" Now he *was* sounding like Mr. Barbuto, itching ears and all.

Lula leaned forward toward the counter. Her child offered a slobbery grin, reminding Oliver of his nephew. "Truth be told, Oliver, you've likely heard that Genevieve's heart was broken something awful by a nefarious individual named Irving. It will be some time before she recovers from her heartbreak."

"Yes, I had heard that."

"Indeed," added Tillie. "Months, maybe even years before her tender heart is fully mended." She closed her eyes and shook her head. "Genevieve is one of the sweetest, most amiable and kindhearted women you will ever meet. Lula and I have a mind to travel to Fentonville and give that rotten nincompoop our thoughts on the matter. While we are most appreciative he did not decide to marry Genevieve, it has left her with a dreadfully, nearly-unrepairable, broken heart."

"I'm sorry to hear that. She received a letter yesterday and..." Oliver recalled Genevieve's slumped shoulders as she trudged slowly down the boardwalk away from the post office.

"We'll check on her," assured Tillie.

Lula tapped her mouth with her finger. "You know, for a bag of jawbreakers, I would share with you a plan that might just remove Genevieve plumb out of her melancholy."

"A bag of jawbreakers?"

"Yes, you know, the ones at the mercantile?"

"Would you be willing to share?" Tillie asked.

Lula tilted her head toward her friend. "Don't I always share the spoils?"

"The spoils?" Oliver asked. "As in spoils from war?"

Tillie laughed. "No, it's how Lula has started to refer to the payment she receives for her extraordinary ideas."

"Extraordinary, indeed. And it'll only cost you a bag of jawbreakers. Mollie knows exactly which ones."

The meager expenditure might be worth finding a way to help Genevieve. "All right. Would you mind informing any customers that my absence is only temporary?"

Tillie confirmed his request, and Oliver crossed the street and sauntered down toward the farthest edge of the boardwalk. Ma would be proud that he had, once again, aided a person in need. How many times had she reminded him to never allow a need to go unnoticed?

"Good morning, Oliver," chirped Mollie as he entered.

"Hello, Mollie. I'm in search of a bag of jawbreakers."

"For Lula?"

"How did you know?"

Mollie laughed. "What plan is she unveiling today?"

Oliver wasn't sure he should share the information, especially since Mollie had paused, a pencil in her hand and a sheet of paper at the ready. This wasn't something that should be printed in the *Ellis Creek Journal.* "Difficult to say," he said.

"Well, Lula has splendid ideas and I'm sure it will be worth the bag of jawbreakers." Mollie retrieved a bag from the shelf and placed it on the counter.

After paying for the candy, Oliver returned the short distance to the post office. He handed Lula the treats.

"I better have one before I present my idea," she said. Adjusting the baby on her hip, she handed the bag of jawbreakers to Tillie, who passed a piece of the candy to both her and Oliver.

Impatience was beginning to set in. It reminded Oliver of when he was a young'un and the teacher announced she had a brand-new assignment for her pupils. Oliver had always loved school and the anticipation and excitement was almost more than he could endure.

"Now for my plan. You see, what Genevieve needs is a dose of cheer, and you, Oliver, can be instrumental in providing that cheer."

"Well, I do try my best to be an affable sort."

Lula reached for her second jawbreaker. "And indeed you are. Now, you two both reside at the boarding house, is that correct?"

"Yes."

"And you both partake in breakfast around Mrs. Vannostrand's mammoth table each morning, correct?"

"Yes." Why did this feel like an interrogation?

Lula and Tillie exchanged glances again. "Every day, leave a note for her at her place setting at the table."

"A note?"

"Yes, a letter of sorts."

Oliver removed his spectacles and placed them on the counter. "I'm not the letter-writing type, Lula."

"But didn't you just say you were an affable sort?"

"Yes, but…"

Lula would have none of his excuses. "Then you exchange pleasantries, only in written form."

"Well said, Lula." Tillie patted her friend's shoulder.

"While I was at the top of my class as a youngster and have always taken to book learning, I'm not a writer."

Lula brushed aside his excuse with a wave of her hand. "No need to be a writer, Oliver. It's not the flowery flow of words that will capture—or, um, rather remove Genevieve's melancholy, but the heart behind those words."

"Ooh, that sounds so inspirational," said Tillie.

"Be inspirational all you want, Lula, I'm not a writer. Now if I need to do a math equation for her, I could do that. I earned high marks in arithmetic."

Tillie lowered her voice as if they were in a clandestine meeting. "Trust us when we say you could do no worse than others who have come before you. Others like Gabe."

"Oh, poor Gabe!" tittered Lula.

While he'd grown up witnessing such foolish drivel in his sisters, Oliver wouldn't ever understand it. He tended to some tasks while he waited for Lula and Tillie to stop their hysterics.

"Honestly, Oliver," Lula continued after attempting to speak without resorting to laughter six times, "you will do just fine. Just a short and thoughtful note each morning, folded so as to avoid the eyes of meddlesome individuals, will serve its purpose well."

"Can you give an example?"

"How about, 'Have a pleasant day, Genevieve?'"

"You don't even have to utilize impressive vocabulary," Tillie added. "Just something encouraging is all that is necessary."

Oliver pondered the idea. Was he even capable of achieving such a task? "How many days am I writing these notes?"

"I'd make an attainable goal to begin with, say a month's worth," Lula suggested.

"A month's worth?" Oliver scratched his head. "I don't think Genevieve will find it helpful to have the same words each morning."

Tillie shook her head. "Not the same words, Oliver. You'll make up a variation of those words each day."

"Are you sure..."

"Just think," said Tillie, "you'll be making a difference in the life of a broken-hearted young woman. A woman who needs your uplifting words to assist her in starting her day with promise."

"There's no guarantee..."

"But you are amenable to the challenge, are you not?" Lula raised her eyebrows, daring him to acquiesce.

How could he not rise to the challenge? "I suppose I could give it a try."

Oliver finished his work tasks and headed to the mercantile for the second time that day. If he was going to leave notes for Genevieve, he should have some stationery. A woman like Genevieve would appreciate letters on something other than scraps of paper or a used envelope.

What length should the notes be? Should he bend the paper in half and fold it into a square? Should he place a cup or a utensil on it to keep it from blowing away in a breeze as someone walked past? What if it fell to the floor before she received it?

His questions overwhelmed him, and Oliver figured he ought to purchase more jawbreakers so he could seek more details from Lula.

"Jawbreakers *and* stationery?" asked Mollie.

She was a pleasant woman, but Oliver heard she had a penchant for fishing for tidbits of news from unsuspecting customers. "Yes."

"Sounds serious."

Oliver paid for his purchases and hoped Mollie wouldn't inquire further.

His hopes were for naught.

"Whenever someone purchases jawbreakers *and* stationery, I find myself a bit suspicious, what with all of the love letters in Ellis Creek over the past years."

Oliver nearly choked on nothing as the air whooshed from him. "Love letters?"

"Why, yes. Gabe and Meredith, Tillie and Will..."

"Oh, I'm *not* writing love letters."

"But you *are* paying Lula in jawbreakers." A glint sparkled in Mollie's eyes.

Oliver did need to write another letter to Ma. He'd promised to write weekly and he'd already missed a week. Didn't bode well for a man who was his ma's favorite son and for one who had easy access to stamps. "I'm from Bozeman and it's about time I wrote to my family."

"You must miss them something terrible."

"I do. My family is close-knit, and I hope to return home for Christmas." Oliver snagged his purchases. "Have a good evening, Mollie."

When he reached the boarding house, Genevieve sat on the bench near the tree, no doubt preparing for tomorrow's school lessons. "Genevieve," he greeted with a nod and touch to the brim of his hat.

"Hello, Oliver."

There was sadness in her blue eyes, but Genevieve's countenance seemed to have improved since yesterday after the distressing letter she received. Would she appreciate the notes he would leave for her? Should he sign his name to them? Oliver checked the hour on his timepiece. Likely suppertime at Lula's house, so not a convenient time to pester her with questions.

Lord, please give me guidance, he prayed as he walked up the narrow stairway to his room. Ma would tell him that whatever he wrote would be a blessing because it was better than no note at all. Pa would tell him to pray, ponder it, and then pray some more. His sisters would goad him until he was seventy about such a featherbrained idea.

Chapter Five

GENEVIEVE JOINED TILLIE, LULA, and Mollie for a lemonade at Lula's house after school the next day. "How are you doing?" Lula asked, passing her a jawbreaker.

If she continued to partake in jawbreakers and lemonade, a trip to the dentist in Fentonville would be in order. "I'm doing better." And she was. As long as she didn't give thought to the letter or mean-spirited Wanda marrying Irving.

"We're so sorry about the letter," said Mollie.

Tillie put on what Genevieve surmised was her best "teacher face". "Now, Mollie, remember. This is not information for the newspaper."

"Thrust aside all of your concerns. I don't write *everything* in the newspaper. I know this is just between the three of us."

Lula placed a kiss atop Baby Jed's head. "And no telling Gid."

Mollie pretended to button her lips. "This secret is safe with me. Gid does know about Irving breaking Genevieve's heart, but nothing more."

"We know the two of you are best friends," added Lula.

Mollie's blue eyes darted around suspiciously. "I don't tell Gid *everything*."

"Just most things?" Tillie asked.

Genevieve joined in the chorus of laughter. It was good to have friends.

"I do tell him a lot of things, but not this. But I will tell you all that I think Mr. Norman fancies Widow Jones."

"And Widow Jones fancies Mr. Norman," added Genevieve.

Mollie nodded. "And if Mr. Norman visits the mercantile for jawbreakers, I am going to be very suspicious." This time Mollie pointed her gaze at Lula.

"I have not heard anything about plans for Mr. Norman to write letters to Widow Jones." Lula popped another jawbreaker in her mouth just as Baby Jed was reaching for the bag. "You're way too little for candies, sweet baby. But when you are older, I'll introduce you to jawbreakers."

"And trips to the dentist," teased Tillie.

Oliver wasted three sheets of paper attempting to write a two-sentence note. Good thing he had taken the time to cut the blue stationery in half so his wastefulness wasn't quite as profound.

Finally, he accepted that what he'd written would have to be sufficient.

He re-read it one more time.

Dear Genevieve,
Have a nice day.

Oliver decided not to sign his name just yet for self-preservation purposes. If Genevieve deemed the letter-writer a cad, then it would be better she not know it was him.

The breakfast bell rang and Oliver folded the note, grabbed his hat, and retreated to the dining area. He needed to arrive at the table before Genevieve, which wasn't an easy feat. If not, he would have to wait until tomorrow morning.

The aroma of fried eggs greeted him. Ma wouldn't have to worry herself that he was getting fed sufficient meals.

Mrs. Vannostrand was an excellent cook and made sure her boarders had more than enough food. He patted his stomach.

Almost too much nourishment.

Thankfully, no one else was at the table yet. He placed the note where Genevieve typically sat—across and one seat over from him.

Pressing it flatter, he tucked the folded note beneath Genevieve's cup, all the while peering about to be sure no one caught him. Oliver chuckled to himself. He hadn't partaken in such clandestine adventures since sneaking a frog into the teacher's desk on a dare when he was ten. "You're the teacher's favorite. No one will know it's you, Oliver," his classmates told him.

No, he wasn't the teacher's first guess, but he did recall the disappointment in her eyes when she discovered he was the culprit. Oliver disliked upsetting people and vowed never again to make it a goal to find new homes for amphibians.

"You're inept at nefarious activity anyway," his oldest sister informed him. "And you have that suspicious face where your expressions betray your emotions and what you're thinking—such as contemplating how you're going to attempt to get away with sneaking frogs into your teacher's desk."

Oliver hoped his "suspicious face with expressions that betrayed his emotions" wouldn't alert anyone to his secret note delivery service. Of course, it likely wouldn't take Genevieve much pondering to decipher who it was leaving the note. A process of elimination was all she would need to do. And it wasn't like Mrs. Crabtree, Mr. Hodgeson, or Adam would leave a note. Perhaps Mrs. Vannostrand or Mrs. Hodgeson might. Those odds were at least in his favor.

"Can I help you with anything?" he asked Mrs. Vannostrand when she zipped around the corner from the kitchen.

"Could you retrieve one more place setting?"

Oliver did as requested, then took his place at the table. And waited.

Mrs. Crabtree, such a grouchy soul with her lack of joy, arrived first. Oliver resisted the urge to nickname her Mrs. Crabby because he'd never met anyone so cranky and irritable.

The woman pulled out Genevieve's chair and took a seat.

Oliver inhaled a sharp breath.

"What do we have here?" Mrs. Crabtree's raspy voice echoed throughout the entire room. Her gnarled fingers proceeded to unfold the note.

"Oh, that's not for you." Oliver bolted from his chair and reached for the note.

But Mrs. Crabtree was faster. She flicked his hand away. "Mind your own business, Mr. Bessell."

"Pardon my saying so, Mrs. Crabb...Crabtree...but that belongs to me."

"Oh, does it now? Who says?"

The woman reminded him more of some of the wayward pupils he recalled from school then a woman of about one hundred and two years old. "Please may I have it?"

Mrs. Crabtree's pointed eyebrow and pressed lips gave evidence of her daring him to bicker with her.

"It is mine, ma'am, and I'm so grateful you found it."

She studied him for a moment and he thought he could see her struggle to relinquish the note. Oliver held his breath.

After several seconds, she hesitantly handed the note to Oliver and he pocketed it.

The other boarders filed into the room. "Good morning, Miss Amsel," Adam announced. Oliver noticed her starting toward the seat directly in front of him. Perhaps she would sit there.

With the quickness of a cheetah, Oliver slipped the note beneath her glass and took a seat before anyone, especially Mrs. Crabtree, who was grumbling about something or other, noticed.

Genevieve retrieved the note and opened it.

And Oliver prayed he wouldn't be obvious.

Chapter Six

GENEVIEVE HADN'T SLEPT WELL the previous night. Thoughts of Irving's refusal to marry her and his willingness to marry Wanda crowded her mind. The anticipation of a wedding with the purchase of her dress, shoes, and earrings—of which she assisted in paying for only to discover the event would never transpire—grieved her all over again.

Yet would she have wanted to be married to Irving? To be married to someone who didn't love her? Whom *she* didn't love?

Conflicting thoughts wrestled in her mind withholding precious time away for sleep. She tossed and turned throughout the night until the scent of pancakes waffled beneath the door the next morning. Stretching and willing her fatigued body to cooperate, Genevieve slid out of bed and prepared for her day, Irving's betrayal heavy on her mind.

When she arrived at the table, Mrs. Crabtree had perched in the chair Genevieve usually sat in, so Genevieve instead settled in the chair next to it across from Oliver. As she placed her cloth napkin into her lap, she noticed a folded pale blue piece of stationery at her place setting. She opened it to find a few words jotted at the uppermost portion of the paper. Genevieve squinted and held it closer to her face to read the minuscule words.

Dear Genevieve,
Have a nice day.

She smiled at the heartwarming gesture and looked around the table at who might have given her the note. The handwriting indicated it was likely a man, and Oliver was the first one who came to mind. Genevieve gazed across the table. Oliver busied himself buttering a piece of bread.

Mr. Hodgeson was the only other male at the boarding house, except for young Adam, whose penmanship was nothing like the tiny scrawled handwriting that nearly required spectacles or a magnifying lens to read.

Yes, it had to be Oliver.

And while she had already come to know him as a congenial and likable man, this confirmed her opinion of him. Such a considerate gesture that meant so much. Six penned words that provided such encouragement.

Until she could thank him properly, Genevieve attempted to catch Oliver's eye. But he proceeded to butter his bread, obviously attempting to ensure every square inch was thickly covered in butter. He was oblivious to her or anyone else around the table. Perhaps she would pretend she didn't know he was the one behind the note.

Genevieve carefully set it to the side of her plate. Oliver's attempt to make her day brighter was most certainly successful.

After breakfast, Genevieve rushed to school. She loved excursions almost as much as her pupils, and today after the noonday meal and recess, they would be visiting the post office to learn about Oliver's occupation.

The morning flew by with arithmetic, writing, and history lessons and the students nearly ran toward the post office in their excitement.

Last week had been a trip to the livery and the week before, a visit to the mill. Next week, they would venture to the bank, and the week after that, the mercantile.

The questions came rapidly as they meandered down the boardwalk.

"Will we all be able to fit inside the post office?"

"Do you think Mr. Bessell remembers we're coming?"

"Will Mr. Bessell allow us to sell some stamps if there's a customer?"

Oliver greeted them just outside the door and Genevieve gave her young scholars their instructions. "Students, please greet Mr. Bessell, who has kindly taken time out of his day to share with us about his occupation."

"Hello, Mr. Bessell," the pupils chorused.

"Now please line up with the shortest in the front and the tallest in the back so we might all crowd into the post office at once."

They did as Genevieve requested and soon the post office was filled with eager children. Genevieve stood at the front just to the side of the counter. Oliver had donned his black postmaster cap that she'd only seen him wear once before. It made him look official. From somewhere in the crowd of children, she heard someone mutter, "Mr. Norman would never have allowed us to gather in such a tiny area." Someone else shushed him and all fell quiet as Oliver began to speak.

"I know many of you were here when Miss Waller, now Mrs. Fairbanks, encouraged you to write letters to Miss Amsel's class in Fentonville, and they, in turn, wrote you back. Delivery of mail has always been a fascinating topic, and today I'm going to share with you how we receive and disburse it."

Enthusiastic murmurs confirmed Oliver's words.

He talked of the journey the mail made and what he did once the mail arrived. Oliver discussed stamps and how youngsters like Adam were valuable helpers when they informed one of the townsfolk they had a letter awaiting them at the post office. He then allowed them to assist in sending a telegram to Fentonville. The visit concluded with questions from the pupils.

Genevieve observed Oliver's camaraderie with her class. He was sure to speak in a way even the youngest understood, but at the same time, was willing to explain in greater detail to the older students. Oliver's convivial and hospitable personality shone in his obligingness and patience with numerous inquiries.

Tillie's words about not all men being like Irving came to mind once again. As her friend insinuated, Oliver Bessell was nothing like Irving.

Indeed. There were no similarities at all.

Oliver borrowed Tillie's thesaurus with the promise he'd take good care of it and wouldn't crease any of the pages or allow any food to be spilled on it. Tillie was so adamant that he take proper care of her favorite book that it surprised him she didn't make him sign a contract indicating he'd guard the tome with his life.

He would need the thesaurus to find words for the notes he planned to leave Miss Amsel and started by looking up the word "happy" and jotting down the synonyms. *Joyous, delightful, jubilant, buoyant, enjoyable, blessed.* That should keep him writing notes for all of...six days. Seven if he included the word "happy".

Oliver sighed. He graduated at the top of his class. He could solve any math problem, recite large portions of the Bible and the entirety of the Declaration of Independence, he understood science, and was an avid historian. He could build things, could train a horse, and could help his pa manage a ranch. And at his job as a postmaster, he prided himself in his ability to decipher most illegible addresses.

But he could not write well.

He somehow needed to make up for that deficiency so he could pen the notes Tillie and Lula suggested he write.

Oliver pondered his dilemma. Perhaps he could change the wording somewhat for the days following the first week of notes. He again flipped open the thesaurus and rifled through the pages. He located the "e" section and looked up the word "enjoy". From there, he wrote on separate pieces of half-sheets of paper the next several days' worth of notes.

Enjoy your day.
Glory in your day.
Revel in your day.
Derive benefit from your day.

All with the same *Dear Genevieve* greeting. He read the notes again. *Derive benefit from your day*? That one would not do.

Back to the thesaurus. And back to his original greeting about what kind of day he wished for Genevieve to have. He added five more notes with the words *pleasant, delightful, splendid, pleasing, and lovely.*

At least he had about two weeks' worth of notes and could ponder the rest in another week or so.

Day two to continue with Tillie and Lula's plan arrived, and Oliver slipped the paper near Genevieve's proposed place setting. But what if Mrs. Crabtree sat there today?

The irritable woman arrived first, as she always did. "Why are you leaving little pieces of folded up paper at my place setting?" she snarled.

"My apologies, Mrs. Crabtree. That belongs at the place setting beside you." He reached for it, grateful for his nimble fingers and speedy reflexes.

"Why are you leaving notes for Miss Amsel?" Mrs. Crabtree pierced him with one of her unblinking glowers and jutted her head forward.

Thankfully, Genevieve and the Hodgesons arrived, averting Mrs. Crabtree's attention. Oliver's eyes darted about the table. No bread today to butter for twenty minutes while Genevieve glanced his way. His expression would snitch on him and he'd never be able to hide the fact he was the one leaving the letters.

He would need to studiously avoid her eye.

Just then an idea miraculously popped into his mind.

After he blessed the meal for the group, Oliver's fork *somehow* fell off the table onto the floor. It was ironic that it fell *just* as Genevieve was unfolding her note.

Oliver bent over to retrieve the fork. Would Genevieve still be looking his way attempting to get his attention after reading the two-second letter?

Likely so. He should wait before returning to his upright position.

He clutched the fork and remained folded for a while longer.

"Ma, where did Mr. Bessell go?" Adam's voice sounded of alarm. "Did he fall under the table?"

"I'm fine, Adam, just getting my fork that fell on the floor," he answered, noting that he was feeling a little lightheaded after being bent over for a couple of minutes.

Finally, he sat up straight, but could see Genevieve's gaze from his peripheral. He stared out the window in the parlor, which only those on his side of the table could see. "The sun is shining brightly today."

"Yes, it is," agreed Mr. Hodgeson.

Oliver remained turned toward the window. "I wonder if there will be a thunderstorm in the afternoon."

"It won't matter what the weather is like outside because you'll be inside still eating your breakfast," barked Mrs. Crabtree.

The heat traveled in a slow wave up his neck and Oliver adjusted his collar. Instead of answering Mrs. Crabtree, he took a bite of his pancakes while keeping his full attention on the plate.

If he had to survive this type of subterfuge every day, he might not be able to execute the plan Tillie and Lula so meticulously laid out for him.

Chapter Seven

GENEVIEVE GRABBED THE TIN pail she'd packed for her noonday meal and started out the door.

"Oliver!"

She'd never known the postmaster to be such a brisk walker.

He stopped and faced her. "Oh, hello, Genevieve. How are you today?"

"I'm well, thank you. And you?"

"I'm well. Say, isn't it a sunny day?"

Why was he acting so peculiar? While they'd only been friends a short time, Genevieve surmised there was a comfort between them as though they'd been friends for years. "Oliver, is something the matter?"

"The matter? No. Why would you ask?" A red tinge covered his face.

"Would you be amenable with me joining you as you walk?"

"Sure. We can walk together."

Always the gentleman, Oliver offered his elbow and she placed her hand through it. Only this time, a strange sensation rippled through her belly. It must have been that she ate her pancakes far too quickly at breakfast. Genevieve ignored it and tended to the matter at hand. "Oliver, I just wanted to thank you for the two notes you've left for me. Such a benevolent gesture."

Oliver stopped and faced her. "I'm not sure I know what you're talking about."

But from the way he avoided her eye and instead studied the ground, it was obvious Oliver Bessell knew exactly what she was talking about. "Oliver, I do know it was you who left me the cheerful notes."

He jerked his head up. "How did you know? Did Mrs. Crabtree tell you?"

"No, she doesn't speak much to me."

"For that you can be grateful." He paused. "Was it my expression? I've been told it always betrays me."

Genevieve giggled. "Well, that may have had something to do with it, but mainly I eliminated all other possibilities and settled on you based on the handwriting."

They continued to walk and passed the barber shop before Genevieve spoke again. "I really appreciate your notes, Oliver. They have brightened my day. Thank you."

"Well, since you've figured out the mystery, you should know I have nearly two weeks' worth of notes left to leave at the breakfast table for you."

"I will appreciate each and every one."

And she would. For Oliver's gracious gesture endeared him all the more to her.

Oliver finished his noonday meal then sat at his desk at the post office to pen his second letter. The first was to ma, and the second was to seek advice. If anyone could aid him with his dilemma, it would be his second-to-the-youngest sister, Lorelei. While he was close to all his sisters, he was closest to her. Besides, his two older sisters were married and his youngest was too young to understand anything about what he intended to ask.

Dear Lorelei,

I hope this finds you doing well. Things here have been busy, but I've finally settled into being the new postmaster at Ellis Creek. I'm sure Ma has shared all of my former letters with you detailing my struggle to convince some of the more obstinate residents that I am fit for the position.

I need your advice. How do I win a young lady's heart? Another man broke her heart so it could be a challenge. How do I convince her I am nothing like him? We haven't known each other for long, but in that time we have become friends. At some juncture, I might consider winning her heart, but have no idea how to do that.

Please keep the contents of this letter between us.

With gratitude,

Your Favorite Brother

Oliver put each of the letters in separate envelopes, purchased two stamps, and tucked them in the mail bag for Gid to take to Fentonville.

He was about to leave for the day when Tillie, Lula, and Baby Jed entered the post office.

"Hello, Oliver," said Tillie. "We came to ask how the note-writing is progressing."

"Well, she guessed it was me after only two notes." Oliver recalled the embarrassment of Genevieve discovering it was him. Her beautiful face flashed through his mind.

Lula shifted Baby Jed in her arms. "That doesn't surprise us. Genevieve is an intelligent woman."

"And I'm not adept at keeping secrets."

"Will you continue to leave notes at her place setting?" Tillie asked.

"Yes. She told me she's appreciated all the ones she's received so far. I hope they encourage her after..." Oliver figured any man who would hurt Genevieve was a scalawag.

Tillie nodded. "After Irving's perfidiousness? Yes, I'm sure your notes have been of great encouragement."

"That's just the problem. I can't think of more than six words to say and the notes are what my oldest sister would refer to as 'mundane'."

Lula tapped her mouth with her finger. "We might be able to help for a bag of..."

"If you let any customers know I'll be right back, I'll go buy those jawbreakers."

Some type of secret glance passed between Lula and Tillie. "Take your time, Oliver. We'll be here when you get back."

Mollie attempted to pry information from him when Oliver purchased the candies. "Need more stationery too?" she asked.

"No, just the jawbreakers." Although, he did only have three sheets left after he used all of the notes he'd written. "Actually, yes, I'll take another box of stationery too."

She tossed him a knowing smirk. "Just as I thought. The same blue or would you prefer a different color?"

"Same blue is fine."

Would Mollie suspect Oliver was growing fond of Genevieve?

He would just have to act nonchalant so she wouldn't get suspicious and write something in the *Ellis Creek Journal*. "I do need to write another letter to my ma and sisters. They'll be expecting me to keep my promise of regular correspondence." Oliver stood up straighter as if that would be more apt to convince her.

"Oh, I see."

Could Mollie see right through Oliver's excuse about purchasing the stationery for his ma and sisters?

The days passed by quickly and Genevieve anticipated receiving Oliver's notes. While they contained few words and were somewhat repetitive, the thought behind them warmed her heart. Her friendship with Oliver grew in the passing weeks and they coordinated their schedules so Oliver could accompany her to work and home on most days. She cherished those times of camaraderie with Oliver and had come to appreciate their rapport.

Genevieve joined the group of residents from the boarding house and moseyed toward the church one Sunday in a relaxed cluster. Clouds loomed in the sky with the threat of rain, but the gentle cooler breeze was a reprieve from yesterday's warmer temperatures. As usual, Mrs. Vannostrand and Adam led the group with Adam bubbling with energy and enthusiasm. Mr. and Mrs. Hodgeson walked together arm in arm beside them and Mrs. Crabtree limped along behind Genevieve. Oliver fell into step beside Genevieve and offered her one of his broad grins—the ones she was becoming so accustomed to.

And while Genevieve would deny it if asked, she had to admit Oliver Bessell was a handsome man.

"Mind if I walk with you?" he asked.

"Not at all."

"Why do you always ask her? Obviously she doesn't mind. You walk together every day. What's so different about Sunday?" Mrs. Crabtree harrumphed, her overly-exaggerated voice conflicting with the otherwise peaceful day.

Oliver said nothing, but lifted his shoulder in a half shrug and tossed a knowing glance Genevieve's way.

They walked in step with each other, Genevieve's hand through the crook of his arm, and Genevieve again marveled at how easy the camaraderie was between them. "Think it will rain again?" he asked.

"I prefer the sunshine myself, but we do need the rain."

"We do. Gabe was talking about how it's been a drier year than usual, which doesn't bode well for the crops and the grasses for the cattle."

"Pshaw. Why do folks always talk about the weather? Besides," grumbled Mrs. Crabtree, "you all walk far too fast. I think I'll just sit down by a tree here by my lonesome and you can enjoy church without me."

Genevieve offered a prayer heavenward for grace toward the disagreeable woman before stopping and turning toward her. "I apologize, Mrs. Crabtree."

The woman bunched her lips and shuffled toward them. "Well, at least someone cares."

Oliver had stopped as well. "May I carry your Bible for you, Mrs. Crabtree?"

"No, you most certainly may not. You are such a presumptuous sort, Mr. Bessell. Always meddling in other people's affairs. Mr. Norman would never have been so impudent."

Presumptuous and impudent would be the last words Genevieve would use to describe Oliver, but she didn't say as much. He was quite the opposite and she found him to be caring and thoughtful. Poor Mrs. Crabtree was so miserable in her bitter state that she didn't realize people only wished to help. Genevieve would do her best to remember to pray often for the woman.

An hour later after the sermon, Reverend Harr mentioned he had a final announcement before everyone left church. "It is my honor to introduce you to Harry Desmond, the owner of the mill, and his sister, Collette Desmond. They are visiting here from Helena for the next few weeks." At the reverend's declaration, a man and woman from the backmost pew stood. "Welcome to our town, Mr. and Miss Desmond."

Outside of the church, Genevieve stood in a circle with Tillie, Lula, and Mollie chatting about their upcoming week when Collette Desmond approached them. "Do you mind if I join you?" The elegant woman in her thirties was dressed in clothing attire more fashionable than anything Genevieve had ever seen in Ellis Creek. Her lavender dress boasted three ruffles on the lower back portion of the skirt, a band that accentuated Collette's slim waist, and white ruffles on the bodice.

"We don't mind at all," said Tillie. "Let me introduce you to everyone. I'm Tillie Fairbanks, and this is Lula Plessner with Baby Jed on her hip. On one side of me is Genevieve Amsel, and on the other, Mollie Reuscher."

"It is delightful to make your acquaintances," said Collette, an oversized smile flashing on her oblong face. "We're only here for two weeks, but with Harry being so dreadfully busy with mill duties, I hope to busy myself with other activities."

"It's delightful to meet you as well," said Genevieve, "And your dress is lovely."

Collette beamed. "Thank you."

They chatted for several minutes, Lula promising to invite Collette to her house one day next week for lemonade, before everyone ventured to their respective homes.

And Genevieve was reminded once again that one of the things she loved about those who resided in Ellis Creek was their gracious and hospitable approach toward newcomers.

Chapter Eight

GENEVIEVE JOINED TILLIE, LULA, Mollie, and Baby Jed outside the bank. They were chatting about a variety of topics when Collette Desmond emerged from the bank.

"Hello, everyone," said Collette, an especially vivacious smile lighting her countenance.

They chorused a greeting and Collette drew closer and lowered her voice. "I have a question about that dapper young man."

Mollie pointed at Gideon who happened to be walking down the street. "You mean Gid?" she asked. Genevieve noticed a sparkle in Mollie's eyes.

"Gid?" Collette frowned. "Oh, no. Not him."

"You mean Mr. Norman?" Tillie asked, nodding toward the elderly former postman who chatted with Widow Jones outside the post office.

"Goodness, but no."

"Who do you mean then?" Genevieve asked.

"That dapper young bank clerk. Such a handsome sort with his mutton chops, fine attire, and piercing eyes." A red flush covered the woman's cheeks. "This is the first time I've had the opportunity to meet him. Do you know if he's spoken for?"

Genevieve watched as Tillie, Lula, and Mollie exchanged glances. She herself had only patronized the bank a handful of times and couldn't recall the names of the employees.

"For a bag of jawbreakers..." started Lula, which resulted in a playful elbow jab from Tillie.

"What she means to say is," started Mollie, "was the man in his thirties with thick eyebrows and even thicker spectacles, a narrow face, and a somewhat beakish nose..."

"Excuse Mollie," said Tillie, "She's the writer for the newspaper and is accustomed to having to provide vivid descriptions."

"That was vivid, all right," agreed Genevieve. She wasn't so sure from the expression on Collette's face if the man in question fit the description. Could it be the wealthy visitor from Helena needed spectacles herself?

Collette alternated her attention from the bank to the women. "He does have thick eyebrows and spectacles. Mostly, what I noticed is that he's quite the dandy."

"I believe you are inquiring about one Mr. Leopold Arkwright III." Tillie adjusted the basket of books she was carrying on her arm. The books that she'd told Genevieve she hoped would be the start of a new library in Ellis Creek.

"The third?" Collette clasped her hands together. "Might he be royalty?"

"Not sure about that," muttered Lula.

The woman's brow creased. "Is Mr. Arkwright's heart spoken for?"

"I don't believe so," said Lula. "He once set his cap for Meredith, Tillie's older sister."

"And now?"

Tillie shook her head. "Meredith has been married for a century to Gabe, so there's no concern there."

Collette pressed a gloved hand to her heart. "That's delightful to hear. Pray tell, what must I do to win the heart of such a distinguished gentleman?"

An amused look passed between Tillie and Lula before Lula spoke. "Perhaps you should make it a priority to frequent the bank on a regular basis while you're visiting Ellis Creek."

"Yes, that is an exceptional idea. He was so charming," Collette swooned. "I do declare that I forgot to ask a question about the availability of funds while I was patronizing the bank a moment ago. Thank you, ladies. Do wish me success in this endeavor." Collette pressed the wrinkles from her skirt and waved at them with a gloved hand before sashaying into the bank once again.

"Oh, dear," said Tillie. "Collette seems like such an affable and cordial woman."

"Much too affable and cordial for the likes of Leopold Arkwright III." Lula pursed her lips as if she'd just eaten something sour.

Mollie shrugged. "What is it they say about beauty being in the eye of the beholder?"

"Indeed," said Genevieve. "I know of whom you speak, although I never knew his name before now."

"He was quite besotted with Meredith. Can you imagine if she would have married him?" Tillie shivered.

Lula shook her head. "We wouldn't have been sisters if Meredith would have chosen him over Gabe."

"I concur," said Mollie. "Good thing you two started your matchmaking society and were able to intervene."

Genevieve had heard of Tillie and Lula's renowned reputation for matchmaking. "Perhaps you could assist Widow Jones and Mr. Norman." She nodded toward the elderly couple who were engaged in conversation near the post office. "They would make a handsome couple."

"From all appearances, they do fancy each other," Tillie said. "I saw him sneak some glances her way during the last church potluck and when we had that barn dance, Mr. Norman asked to dance with her for nearly all of the dances."

Mollie chewed on her lip. "Perhaps they are just long-time friends. Sometimes that's all folks are is friends and they're not interested in courtship."

"Hmm." Tillie and Lula exchanged one of their secretive glances. "Perhaps."

"What about you and Oliver, Genevieve?" Mollie nodded toward the post office where Oliver had emerged.

"I... no, I learned my lesson about courtship when Irving broke my heart."

Tillie squeezed Genevieve's arm. "That odious man did not deserve you."

"A scoundrel for sure," agreed Lula.

"Thank you, Tillie and Lula. I definitely won't be falling in love again after that incident."

"Who can blame you?" asked Tillie. "I would be the same way."

Genevieve watched as Oliver greeted everyone he passed on the boardwalk. If only the situation with Irving hadn't happened the way it had. If only they'd parted on amicable terms.

Perhaps then she would be able to open her heart to someone like Oliver.

Oliver tapped his pencil on the desk. Tillie and Lula encouraged him to begin writing more detailed notes just when he'd become proficient at writing numerous short ones with few words. What would Genevieve think when, after a month and a half, the letters changed?

Likely he wouldn't have to worry about her thoughts on the matter because the words would just not come to him.

He unfolded Lorelei's response and read it again.

Dear Oliver,

So good to hear from you. I'm sorry about some of the residents not being as accepting. Perhaps they need a chance to become better acquainted with you. When they do, I'm confident they will fully welcome you.

I've been busy working at my new position at the Bozeman library. We are on the second floor of the city hall building. Currently there have not been many patrons, but I do hope in time that will change.

As for winning a young lady's heart, your particular scenario does present more of a challenge than most, what with the woman's heart having been broken. She likely believes all men are rapscallions like the man who broke her heart. It will be up to you to prove you are different. I know I would be endeared to thoughtful gestures. Perhaps spending time with

her will give her the evidence she needs to see you are a
kindly gentleman.

I will keep your inquiry just between us.

Do write and tell me how you fare.

Yours truly,

Your Favorite Second-to-the-Youngest Sister

Oliver already did spend time with Genevieve and had for the past several weeks. They often chatted outside on the porch or on the bench beneath the oak tree. They walked together most mornings and sat across from each other at breakfast and supper. He'd written her notes, which he would consider a thoughtful gesture, and would now endeavor to write more substantial ones.

He stood at the window. The sunset, as always, was glorious with its hues of orange and purple. But as much as he might want to spend time gaping at it, if he wasn't careful it would be tomorrow. And by tomorrow morning, he needed another note or letter or something to leave at Genevieve's place setting. Oliver didn't want to disappoint her by missing a day.

With a sigh, he again focused on the blank sheet of paper before him. The words of his heart began to flow, but Oliver knew from the second his pencil commenced to scribbling, this would be a letter that Genevieve would never receive.

Dear Genevieve,

I believe I am falling in love with you. Each evening after we part ways, I find that I can't wait until the following day to spend time with you again. Our talks, walks, and time spent together has further anchored my feelings for you. I know Irving hurt you when he decided not to marry you. He was a fool to make that decision. You have my word that I would never hurt you and if given the chance, would love you forever.

You have a strong faith and your love for Jesus is apparent. You are a patient teacher with your pupils and a compassionate woman. I appreciate your grace toward Mrs. Crabtree, which isn't an easy feat.

I have grown fond of your smile and the way your blue eyes light up when you are happy about something. I like your laugh and your wit. I've never met a prettier woman than you.

I hope to someday have a chance to win your affections.

Yours truly,

Oliver

Lorelei would deem him smitten for sure.

Of course, he would never give the letter to Genevieve. What would she think of him declaring his love for her? Likely that he was a buffoon.

So instead, Oliver wrote another note just like all the other ones he'd left for her before.

Chapter Nine

OLIVER FINISHED PENNING SOMETHING in the ledger when he peered out the window just in time to see Gideon parking in front of the mercantile, down a ways and catty-corner from the post office. Oliver squinted. Could it be his anticipated delivery on the back of Gideon's freight wagon? Oliver set his pencil and spectacles on top of the ledger, removed his white postmaster's apron, and bolted from the post office.

Gideon was unloading crates and placing them on the boardwalk. Oliver resisted the temptation to leap onto the back of the wagon and retrieve his order.

Patience, grasshopper, Ma would always say whenever he was overly eager. But today with the shiny order begging him to remove it and relive wonderful days of the past, being a "patient grasshopper" was not something Oliver was sure he could achieve.

"Hello, Gid!"

Gideon propped a shovel against the outside wall of the mercantile. "Hello, Oliver. Reckon you're here to retrieve your purchase."

"You reckoned right." Oliver wiped his sweaty palms on his trousers. The expense of the sleek new item had set him back some as far as funds went, but he hoped—no, he knew—it would be worth it.

"Few more things to unload before I can get to it."

"Can I help?"

"Sure thing."

Oliver assisted Gideon with removing several crates, a bag of mail, and a few farm implements before Gideon jumped into the back of the wagon and wheeled Oliver's purchase to the edge. "It's a beaut," he said, lifting it from the wagon.

But Gideon didn't set it on the ground immediately.

Oliver could barely contain the urge to tap his foot on the ground. What was the delay? His answer came quickly when he noticed Gideon staring at something—or rather, someone—a few feet away. Oliver's purchase rested in Gid's arms, suspended in midair.

Mollie giggled at something a customer was saying as they stood just inside the door of the mercantile.

As though mesmerized, Gid gaped in Mollie's direction as though he'd never seen her before.

"Uh, Gid?"

"Yeah?" But Gid kept his focus on Mollie. Only someone with the strength Gideon possessed could stand holding something somewhat heavy and awkward in such a fashion.

"Could you set that on the ground?"

"Set what?"

Gid was acting as though he was smitten with Mollie, when in fact, from what Tillie said, the two were best friends. Oliver glanced in her direction. She looked the same as always. "You might quit staring at Mollie and set that on the ground. It's hard to be patient and all while you're standing there in a discombobulated state.

"Uh, oh, yes, sure, Olive—er—Oliver."

"Yes, Oliver, not Olive." Oliver moved to stand directly in front of Gideon. While he was an inch or two shorter and not as hefty, he could manage to block Gid's view temporarily. But his friend peered around him.

Finally, Oliver reached for the item and eased it to the ground.

"Sorry about that, I was just..."

"Staring at Mollie?"

Gideon's eyes bugged and his face took on a reddened hue. "Maybe."

"You see her every day."

"Yes, but..." Gid turned around and finished unloading a few smaller items from the wagon.

And Oliver ran his hand over the sleek black frame of his new bicycle. Well, not new, because he could never afford something new. But this fantastic invention, a used one Pa had stumbled across in Bozeman and that had been delivered all the way to Fentonville and then to Ellis Creek, was all his.

"Nice contraption," Gid said after Mollie disappeared from his vision.

"That it is. It's an 1889 Overman safety bicycle built by the Overman Wheel Company in Boston." Oliver stooped to investigate the spokes and pedals.

Gid's brow furrowed. "Why would someone such as yourself need a bicycle?"

"Have you ever tried one of these?"

"Can't say as I have. I'm more of a horse man, myself."

Oliver patted the wooden seat. "Horses are fine, but a bicycle can give you a different kind of freedom. It's an impressive invention, what with its all-steel body and hollow tires. And when you're going fast enough, it's what I imagine flying would feel like. On the ground, of course. Bicycles are popular in cities where folks ride them often. There are even bicycle clubs and such."

"I doubt there will be bicycle clubs anytime soon in Ellis Creek."

"Maybe not, but you really will have to try this, Gid."

Oliver climbed on the seat and positioned his hands on the handlebars. "Think I might try it right here rather than waiting until this evening at the boarding house."

He pushed himself to the side of the wagon with his feet before beginning to pedal down the road.

He observed several townsfolk stop their activities and gape at him as he rode his bicycle down the main part of town toward the schoolhouse. The breeze caught the sleeves of his shirt and Oliver pedaled a little faster. It was exactly as he recalled in Bozeman before moving to Ellis Creek. He'd borrowed his friend's bicycle and had vowed then to someday own this fine mode of transportation.

And while it cost him a pretty penny, it would be worth it to ride it back and forth between the short distance between the boarding house and the post office and even for a pleasant weekend ride.

Oliver rounded the corner halfway to the Wallers' house, then turned around, lest he be gone too long from his commitment at the post office. He waved at several passersby and rode past Lula and Jed's and on the way to the school where the children were at recess.

He spied Genevieve from a distance, her beauty taking him aback as it always did whenever he saw her. Oliver chuckled to himself. He likely resembled Gid from a few minutes earlier when he'd seen Mollie.

Genevieve turned toward him, paused for a moment, then lifted her hand to wave. Oliver waved back and steered the bicycle toward where she stood at the base of the school steps. Several children ran to greet him, their questions coming at a rapid pace.

"What is that, Mr. Bessell?"

"Can I try it?"

"Did you buy that from the mercantile?"

"Is that one of those newfangled bicycles?"

Oliver proceeded to answer the myriad of questions before focusing his attention on Genevieve.

"I've seen one of those before in Fentonville," she said.

"My best friend in Bozeman had one he allowed me to ride on occasion. That's when I knew I would own one of my own someday."

Genevieve's blue eyes sparkled. "Might I try it sometime?"

"How about after school?"

With the smile she gave him, he would *give* her the bicycle. "I would like that," she said. "Is it easy to learn?"

Oliver shrugged. "It takes practice to become skilled at balancing, but once you learn, you don't forget. The boarding house would be a perfect place to try it."

"I shall see you then at the boarding house after school." She tossed him one more smile and Oliver was reminded once again that he was falling in love with the beautiful teacher, even if she didn't feel the same for him. He could hardly blame her after what that scoundrel Irving did.

Several of the students crowded around them.

"Can we come too, Mr. Bessell?"

"May I try your bicycle?"

"Does it go really fast?"

"Can it go faster than a horse?"

Oliver chuckled at the curiosity of the pupils. They reminded him of his young niece and nephew. "Yes, you may all stop by the boarding house after I'm relieved of my duties at the post office. And yes, the eldest of you may try the bicycle. It goes reasonably fast, but not faster than a horse. Its speed depends on how rapidly you pedal."

Lest he remain stranded at the school and neglect his postmaster duties, Oliver bid farewell to Genevieve and the students and rode back to the post office. Hopefully there had been no customers during his brief time away. He parked the bicycle on the boardwalk out of the way of passersby and entered the post office, only to find Mr. Bellinger hunched over the counter. "Where have you been?" the man growled.

"I had to take my leave for a brief moment."

"On that thing out there with wheels?"

"Yes, sir, it's known as a bicycle."

"Don't care none what it's known as. All I know is that you left the post office open and with no one here to oversee it." Mr. Bellinger pointed a crooked finger at him. "Mr. Norman would never do that. He'd never leave the post office unoccupied and without a clerk. How they ever thought you were fit for this job is beyond me."

Oliver had heard Mr. Bellinger's complaints so often that they no longer affected him the way they once had. Still, he had to bite his tongue to avoid retorting something Ma would say wasn't becoming of a young Christian man. Instead, Oliver prayed for the right words, took a deep breath, and spoke. "With all respect, sir, I only left for a few minutes. Now I'm back. How may I assist you?"

Mr. Bellinger narrowed his eyes. "Just because you were educated at some fancy school don't mean you need to talk all fancy-like. This is Ellis Creek, not Missoula where you hail from."

"Bozeman, sir. I'm from Bozeman." Oliver wouldn't waste time arguing with Mr. Bellinger about his education. And while he appreciated book learning, had read every book he could obtain, and prided himself on working the most challenging of mathematical equations, Oliver had never attended a fancy school.

"Bozeman, Missoula, what's the difference?"

"Now then, Mr. Bellinger, what brings you to the post office on this otherwise pleasant morning?"

Mr. Bellinger coughed and cleared his throat three or four times as particles of spittle flew from his mouth and landed on the counter. "I'm in need of a stamp and can you see if I got myself any mail?"

Oliver removed a stamp from the drawer and checked the mail slots. "I don't see any, but I do know that Gideon just arrived with the mail bag and I will be sorting that posthaste."

"I'm waiting for a letter from my daughter. She lives in Kansas City, Missouri, where she moved with her husband."

Mr. Bellinger lived an hour from town on the way to Fentonville or Oliver would have offered to stop by his home later if he discovered there was, in fact, a letter for the man. "If you have some errands in town, I will be starting on the mail bag right after the noonday meal."

"Or you could check the bag right now." Mr. Bellinger attempted to straighten his posture, although he still remained severely stooped.

"Oliver, sometimes folks don't deserve our kindness, but it's oftentimes those folks who need it the most." Ma's words entered his mind. Mr. Bellinger always complained whenever he visited and had even written a letter to Oliver's superiors requesting he be immediately removed from his post.

"It's not always easy to do the things the Lord would have us do, Son. Sometimes what we want and what we should do contradict each other." This time, Pa's words emerged in Oliver's thoughts.

Both Ma and Pa were correct and Oliver knew what needed to be done.

He located the mail bag off to the side of the counter and opened it. Pilfering through the letters, he searched for one addressed to Mr. Bellinger. There was a letter to just about everyone else in town, but no mail for the man scowling at him.

"I'm sorry, sir, but there are no letters for you today."

"Nonsense!" he slammed his wrinkled fist on the counter, more spittle flying from his mouth. "Check again."

Oliver didn't appreciate Mr. Bellinger's rude behavior and almost refused to do his bidding, but when he saw a tear emerge in the depths of the man's eyes, he changed his mind. No, Mr. Bellinger didn't deserve Oliver's kindness, but he likely needed it the most. Oliver lifted the bag to the counter and took out the pile of letters and leafed through them again. Mr. Bellinger's mouth moved silently as he read the recipient of each one.

"I'm sorry, sir, but there are no letters for you today," Oliver repeated, being sure to keep his tone respectful.

"Why hasn't she written? It's been far too long since I heard from her."

"Sometimes the mail takes longer to be delivered than we'd like."

Mr. Bellinger lowered himself on the counter, giving Oliver a full glimpse of his balding head covered with a smattering of brown moles. He'd folded his wrinkled hands, his head bowed.

Oliver waited until the man finished praying before he spoke again, his voice low. "Sir, if I receive a letter for you and it's not on the day you come to town for errands, I will personally deliver it to you."

The man lifted his head and eyed Oliver with suspicion. "Why would you do that?"

"Because it's important to you." *And because I've tasted God's mercy and grace and will, with some hesitation, do my best to extend the same to you.*

"Don't trouble yourself." Mr. Bellinger turned on his heel and shuffled from the post office.

Leaving Oliver to wish he'd received the expected letter for one of his most difficult customers.

Chapter Ten

AFTER DISMISSING SCHOOL, GENEVIEVE finished her schooling duties and closed the door behind her. The sunny day beckoned her and she briefly tilted her face toward the sky. "Too much sun will most certainly give you freckles. Only those of low society would allow freckling on their skin," Aunt Blanche would say.

Genevieve shoved her aunt's warnings aside and allowed the warmth to settle on her face. While she'd not stay there long enough to procure freckling, she wouldn't allow memories of Aunt Blanche's constant concerns to ruin her day.

After a few moments, she started down the steps. Genevieve clutched the schoolbooks to her chest and thought about the assignments she would find within them for her pupils for tomorrow's lessons. When she first moved to Ellis Creek, Tillie taught with her for a short time, but then Tillie married Will and the town hired another teacher to assist in tending to the increasing population. Now Tillie tutored those who struggled with their book learning and needed extra assistance.

And Genevieve had settled right into the town she now called home. Over time, her heart had begun to heal from Irving's betrayal and she'd made many friends in Ellis Creek.

Oliver's face flashed through her mind. He had been an especially thoughtful friend with the notes he left at the breakfast table at the boarding house.

Genevieve walked the distance to the boarding house, waving at passersby as she did so. When she approached the area near the bench and the oak tree, she noticed her pupils had already gathered, eagerly awaiting Oliver's arrival.

"Hello, Miss Amsel, have you seen Mr. Bessell yet?" Lula's daughter, Theodora, asked.

Several other students murmured excitedly. "I wonder if he'll think I'm old enough to ride the bicycle. He said only the eldest."

"He's a nice man. My ma and pa like Mr. Norman better, but I like Mr. Bessell better."

Genevieve agreed with her student's musings. She thought Oliver was nice as well and she found herself looking forward to seeing him every day. And while a bit nerve-wracking, she was eagerly anticipating trying the new bicycle herself. "I'm sure he'll be here shortly. It is just about time for him to conclude his day at the post office."

Little Gabe handed Genevieve a piece of paper. "I drawed a picture of Mr. Bessell's bicycle."

Genevieve perused the youngster's sketch. "This is quite impressive, Little Gabe."

A smile lit the boy's face. "Thank you, Miss Amsel. See here, this is the seat and these is the handlebars. And this is me riding it." He pointed to a portrait of a grinning child, his smile nearly as big as his face. Little Gabe had talent and had captured his own likeness well.

"Look! It's Mr. Bessell!" Three of the children started running toward Oliver as he rode toward them.

Oliver removed a hand from the handlebars and waved at them. Several students trailed after him, laughing and asking more questions.

He stopped near the tree and leaned the bicycle against it. The students crowded around him all speaking at once. Oliver patiently visited with the children before placing Little Gabe on the seat. The boy's feet dangled and he giggled as Oliver pushed him slowly along the road.

And something in Genevieve stirred as she witnessed the interaction.

She was fortunate to have found a friend in such a kind and gentle man.

After several of the children took their turns, Oliver approached her. "And for you, Miss Amsel, would you care for a ride on the infamous Overman Wheel Company safety bicycle?" He pretended to remove a hat and took a bow.

"Why thank you, kindest of sirs."

The children laughed and Theodora repeated Genevieve's words. "The kindest of sirs," she said, eliciting another round of laughter.

Genevieve inspected the bicycle from a close distance and ran her hand along the triangular-shaped brown seat with four curly spring coils beneath it.

"The Victor Safety is the finest of all bicycles," Oliver said, stepping beside her. His shoulder brushed hers and Genevieve's heart beat a little faster.

It obviously was because she was sharing in his excitement of the bicycle.

Oliver smoothed his hand along the black frame. "These modes of transport are expensive when new, but my pa was able to secure this used one for me at a reasonable cost."

Genevieve had seen such bicycles in the newspaper in Fentonville and her uncle had even spoken of purchasing one for himself. But she'd never seen one in person.

"And much safer than the penny farthing," Oliver was saying.

She turned her gaze to him and witnessed once again the enthusiasm in his expression. His mouth turned up at the corners and his voice was light. He spoke quickly as he described all of the benefits of the Overman in contrast to the tall high-wheeled bicycles boasting a larger wheel in front and a smaller one in the back. "Those were dangerous," said Oliver. "Lofty and unstable. I recall seeing a gentleman ride one in Bozeman years ago and he broke both of his wrists attempting to protect himself when he fell off it."

The children offered their commentary.

"That sounds scary, Mr. Bessell."

"Were the man's wrists all right?"

"Just how tall was the penny farthing?"

"Is this bicycle dangerous too?"

Genevieve contemplated the last inquiry. Should she attempt the feat of riding the bicycle?

"I will be right here to steady you," Oliver said, as if to read her mind.

He stood to one side and gestured toward the bicycle. "Might I assist you?" he asked, with another bow and this time feigning a British accent.

Genevieve lifted her chin and said in her own British accent, "Most certainly and absolutely."

Oliver helped her onto the bicycle. "Your hands go here," he instructed, and Genevieve placed her hands on the handlebars. Oliver steadied her by resting his own hand on the steering bar, his fingers briefly touching hers.

A flutter took up residency in her stomach and she assumed it was due to the nerves she was experiencing from trying a bicycle for the first time.

In ladylike fashion, Genevieve perched atop the seat, grateful the lower bar of the bicycle did not impede her movements.

She pedaled as Oliver instructed and he walked along beside her, helping her to balance.

"It's a whole new world of freedom," Oliver said.

The wisps of hair that had fallen from Genevieve's chignon fluttered back away from her face with the breeze as she pedaled slightly faster.

"What do you think?" Oliver asked.

"I'm enjoying it immensely." And she was.

Oliver continued to walk along beside her, keeping her steady. She glanced briefly at him and noticed, perhaps for the first time, his broad shoulders. His strong forearm supported her and she reveled in both the independence of riding the bicycle coupled with the reassurance that with Oliver beside her, all would be well.

What would her aunt say if she could see Genevieve at this very moment?

But there was nothing unladylike or unrefined about Genevieve riding the bicycle and from what she'd read in *The Fentonville Courier*, women frequently rode bicycles in large cities.

She teetered a bit, but overall was impressed with her swift learning ability.

"You're doing fantastic, Miss Amsel. Shall I release my hold on the steering bar?"

"Perhaps for a brief moment, Mr. Bessell."

After all, she was doing quite well balancing.

And then the most embarrassing thing happened. There was a slight slant in the road and Genevieve dipped along, bouncing slightly on the seat. The bicycle began to go faster. "Oliver?"

"I'm right here, you're doing great, Genevieve."

The bicycle went even faster and she attempted to steer around a large pothole in the road. "Oliver?"

"I'm coming! Stop pedaling, Genevieve."

She heard his footsteps as she struggled to maintain control of the wayward mode of transportation.

The handlebars wiggled and Genevieve tottered. Her heart raced. She held her feet still, but the bicycle continued to trek along at a fast speed. "Oliver!"

He was beside her then, his hand on the handlebars near her own hand, attempting to steady her. "Use the brake," he said.

She tried to do as he commanded, she really did, but she wobbled and swayed and wobbled and swayed some more. Oliver ran alongside her. Finally, he reached over and steadied her once again. "Thank you," she gasped.

The bike lurched forward and she heard footsteps behind them. The children, perhaps?

It was about that time that Genevieve came upon another dip in the road. A wheel skidded against the dirt road, the bicycle tipped, and Genevieve fell right into Oliver.

"Oh, dear!"

The next thing she knew, Oliver's arm was around her and her feet were tangled in the bicycle.

"Just a minute, I'll remedy this," he said.

Genevieve closed her eyes and willed her racing heart to settle.

"Just step over the bicycle," Oliver said.

She did so, and was finally unhooked from the Overman.

"Are you all right, Genevieve?"

She blinked, observing that she rested firmly against Oliver and that his arm remained around her. "Oh. I. Yes."

His gaze met hers and she peered into his tender pale green eyes. Such handsome eyes with rings of vivid navy blue around the pupils. Not that she was noticing.

Her heart pounded and she wondered if he could hear it.

"I'm thankful you are all right. You could have been hurt," he said, his voice low.

They stood there for the briefest of moments, Genevieve leaning into Oliver all the while a ribbon of excitement twirled in her belly. His face was so close to hers. She attempted to brush aside the thought that she rather liked being tucked into his arm—almost as if she belonged there—but the thought would not depart from her mind. She closed her eyes briefly and inhaled a pleasant combination of paper and ink.

"I...uh..." Oliver removed his arm from around her shoulder.

His voice distracted her from her musings about the comfort of resting in his arms. "Oh, dear," she said and pulled away, pressed the wrinkles from her skirt, and nodded toward the children who were asking ninety questions a second.

"Miss Amsel! Miss Amsel! Did you break both of your wrists?"

"Was riding the bicycle fun despite tipping over, Miss Amsel?"

"Are you going to try riding it again? Pa always says to always try again even if you fail the first time."

"I reckon we should reassure the children all is well," said Oliver. A smirk lit his face.

And as Genevieve stood there attempting to right herself after her adventure, she reminded herself to exercise caution.

Because if she didn't, she could very well lose her heart to Oliver Bessell.

Chapter Eleven

THE FOLLOWING DAY, GENEVIEVE met Tillie at her house after school and after Tillie had finished her tutoring appointment. Tillie poured them each a cup of lemonade then took a seat across from Genevieve at the table. "I have the most extraordinary news to share," Tillie said.

"Yes?" She leaned toward her friend.

Tillie's eyes brightened. "Will and I are going to have a baby."

"Congratulations!" Genevieve hugged her friend. "I'm so happy for you."

"Thank you. Only a handful of people know—you, Will, my parents, Meredith, my brother, and Lula."

Genevieve's eyes misted. "I'm thrilled for you."

"If you would have asked me not too far in the distant past if I would have ever imagined being married to Will and soon to be a mother, I would have answered with an astounding, 'no', but now...thank you for sharing in my excitement, Genevieve." Tillie paused and took a sip of her lemonade. "Now, do tell me all about this matter with Oliver's bicycle. I heard it was quite the adventure."

"Oh, it was. Oliver brought his new bicycle to the boarding house where he allowed some of the older children to ride it. Then it was my turn. All was well until I realized it really is true that pride goeth before a fall. Quite literally, I might add." Genevieve laughed. "Who knew I would be riding one at all. I can only imagine what my aunt would say if she knew."

"But it is the latter part of the century and women do ride bicycles, especially in the cities."

"Indeed. And I recall reading an article in the Fentonville newspaper about that very topic."

Tillie propped her chin on her hands. "So, what happened after you realized you couldn't ride as well as you thought?"

"I tipped over, but thankfully, Oliver was there to steady me."

Tillie's eyes grew large. "Oliver was there to steady you? And did you fall into his arms?"

"Now, Tillie, do not think that..."

"That you might be fond of Oliver?"

Genevieve shook her head. "He is a nice, gentle, and kind man. He loves the Lord and has a sparkling wit, but he and I are merely good friends."

"Would it be so wrong to be fond of Oliver?"

"Now, Tillie, you know full well that I will never allow myself to fall in love again."

Tillie's eyebrows raised into her forehead. "Could you be so sure of that?"

"I'm sure." But even as she uttered the words, Genevieve knew she might not be able to keep that promise.

"I realize that Irving hurt you badly, but Oliver is not Irving."

Genevieve would be remiss if she denied having compared the two men. "True. But I can't risk another broken heart."

But the words sounded hollow in Genevieve's ears. Could it be possible she *was* growing fond of Oliver?

Oliver rested his fishing pole on the banks of the Ellis Creek and took a seat on the boulder beside Mr. Norman. He unwrapped the sandwich Mrs. Vannostrand prepared for him and took a bite after the older man blessed the meal.

Mr. Norman ate his own sandwich, then retrieved a tin of cookies and handed Oliver one. "Widow Jones made these. Mighty delicious if I do say so."

"Widow Jones?"

"Her grandson delivered them to me yesterday afternoon." Mr. Norman bit into one of the cookies. He closed his eyes and shook his head. "That woman sure knows how to bake. Reckon if you weren't sitting here, I'd eat the whole lot all by myself."

"I didn't realize Widow Jones made cookies for you."

A tinge of red covered the man's wrinkled face. "She's a thoughtful sort. Purdy too."

Oliver raised an eyebrow. Did Mr. Norman fancy the widow? There was speculation among the townsfolk that that was the case.

Mr. Norman cleared his throat. "Fine day for fishing, but then every day is a fine day for fishing."

"I couldn't have said it better. My pa used to take us fishing frequently."

"You miss your family, don't you, son?"

Oliver thought of his parents and sisters in Bozeman. "I do. They've been contemplating moving to Fentonville for the last several years. I'm hoping to help them in their decision as then they'd be closer to Ellis Creek."

"A man can't do much better than a good family." Mr. Norman took another bite of his cookie, and Oliver noticed only a few more remained in the tin.

"Where are my manners? Care for another?"

"No, thank you. Mrs. Vannostrand packed me some fruit along with two sandwiches."

Mr. Norman nodded. "I recall when I was young'un. Things were different back then. 'Course, I spent my growing-up years in Indiana on a farm."

"What brought you to Ellis Creek?"

"The postmaster job. I came to Montana and never looked back."

Oliver had never lived anywhere but Montana, and he was proud to call the state his home. His thoughts took a different route. "The townsfolk sure do miss you as their postmaster."

"It was an enjoyable job and the one the Lord led me to. I met a lot of interesting folks over the years of being a postmaster both here and in a couple of other towns in Montana. I enjoyed it, but I don't miss it. There's too many fish to be caught for me to be sorting through mail all day." Mr. Norman's low amusing rumble caused Oliver to chuckle too.

Most of the folks in Ellis Creek were kind and gracious and many had become Oliver's friends, but there were some that struggled with adjusting to someone other than Mr. Norman as their postmaster. Oliver stared out over the sparkling water. "In my first few days here, I'd contemplated quitting and returning home to Bozeman." His mouth uttered the words before he could give them thought.

Mr. Norman placed a hand on his shoulder. "It's never easy to follow in the steps of a predecessor. But you're doing a fine job as the new postmaster, Oliver. Sometimes, people, especially the older ones and myself included, can get set in their ways a bit. We don't like change."

"I just want to be able to serve the people of Ellis Creek."

"And you are. You're serving them with integrity and hard work. No one can ask for more than that. You don't open letters addressed to others or snoop into other people's business like some postmasters."

Oliver thought of Mr. Barbuto in Bozeman. "No, I would never do that." He reached for the second sandwich from his tin pail. "Do you have any other wise words of wisdom you can offer me?"

"About the best advice I can give you is to continue to ask the Lord for guidance. And then just keep doing exactly what you have been doing because people will come to their senses."

"Thank you, Mr. Norman."

"You're welcome. Now what say we commence to some more fishing while it's still daylight."

Oliver considered Mr. Norman's words about his job as a postmaster. He'd made several friends here in Ellis Creek in the short time he'd been here. Genevieve's face flashed through his mind.

His ambitions for Ellis Creek were twofold. That someday he would be able to prove to the townsfolk he was worthy of the postmaster position. And secondly, that he would be able to convince Genevieve he was nothing like the man who broke her heart.

Oliver left the boarding house the following morning, ready to face the day. The sun shone brightly and the birds happily chirped. Not a cloud filled the sky and the mountains in the distance with their tall peaks rose above the lower valleys in grand majesty. It was one of those days where nothing could possibly go awry. Oliver climbed on his bicycle and pedaled down the street and toward the post office. He whistled a tune as he passed by other businesses on his way to the post office.

Genevieve filled his mind, as she oftentimes did. Lorelei would tell him he was captivated by her.

And perhaps he was. For although he'd appreciated her friendship first, it had grown to more in the months of knowing her.

The boardwalk was nearly empty save for Mrs. Crabtree who'd started out before him from the boarding house. She shuffled along, hunched over and clutching her cane, with her reticule dangling off her opposite arm. He could only see her from the back, but from past experience being in her presence, Oliver imagined Mrs. Crabtree's brow was furrowed and her mouth was set in a straight firm line. The poor woman lived up to her name and he'd never, not once, seen a smile on her wrinkled face. Never, not once in the time he'd spent at the boarding house had he seen her do anything but overtly challenge whatever anyone else said, and not in the gentlest of tones.

Ma would remind him to pray for Mrs. Crabtree, and Oliver figured she needed many prayers.

Just as he was contemplating how he could make a habit of praying for the ill-tempered woman, out from nowhere, a man emerged. He ran toward Mrs. Crabtree, bumped into her, nearly knocking her off her feet. And then in an expedient moment, one that Oliver would not have believed had he not seen it for himself, the man grabbed Mrs. Crabtree's reticule and bolted down the boardwalk.

"Help! Someone help! That man stole from me!"

He stopped next to the woman. "Mrs. Crabtree, are you all right?"

"Pshaw, young man. I'm perfectly fine. Now do go after that bandit and retrieve my reticule."

"Yes, ma'am."

Already halfway down the boardwalk, the man secured an advantage over Oliver. Without wasting another second, Oliver pedaled faster, knowing that if he hurried, he could still catch the thief.

His legs welcomed the exertion. The freedom. The thrill of riding the Overman at a faster rate of speed than his usual leisurely rides. But as much as he welcomed that freedom, Oliver knew that if he was to catch the man, he'd have to increase his speed all the more.

"Stop that man!" he called to the few passersby. Instead of preventing the man from continuing down the boardwalk, folks stood in place with shocked expressions on their faces.

Likely puzzled that there could be anything amiss in the peaceful town of Ellis Creek.

Oliver pedaled faster, the slight breeze blowing past him, and his eyes trained on the thief. Would he be successful in stopping him? Should he instead turn around and go in the opposite direction toward the sheriff's office? After all, Oliver was not a trained member of the law.

His heart pounded wildly in his chest. The man was still in his sights when the crook crossed the street in front of an oncoming wagon, narrowly meeting his demise. The wagon stopped, but the thief dashed into the narrow alleyway between the livery and blacksmith.

Oliver veered into the alley. He hunched over the handlebars and willed his legs to go faster. Thankful for exceptional balance, Oliver pressed on, bridging the distance between him and the thief.

The man turned his head at just that moment and spied Oliver. Instead of heeding his surroundings, he collided with a barrel and fell to the ground.

Now was Oliver's chance.

Just as the man stood and was about to run again, Oliver angled the bicycle in front of him, effectively halting his movement. And then, in a maneuver that would likely impress the ringmaster in one of those circuses back East Oliver had heard about, he leapt off his bike and tackled the man to the ground.

He may not be large and muscular like Gid, but he *was* swift and nimble.

"Leave me be!" shouted the man.

"Just hand over the reticule."

"Don't got no reticule."

"The one in your hand."

There was a pause and then an uttered, "Oh, that one."

"Best do as he says and then we'll be hauling you to jail." Oliver glanced up to see the Ellis Creek sheriff standing over them. "Good job, Oliver. I'll handle the matter henceforth."

Genevieve stood beside Oliver in front of the church where a crowd had gathered around. Today the entire town would honor him for his bravery in nabbing the thief who stole Mrs. Crabtree's reticule. Folks had already congratulated him many times over for his courageous act before quieting to hear Reverend Harr's announcement.

"I never imagined I'd be chasing a criminal on the Overman," Oliver said, a broad grin alighting his face.

Their eyes met and Genevieve's heart jolted. His green eyes were greener than usual today, likely because of his plaid green shirt. "No, I imagine not. Were you terribly nervous about chasing and apprehending him?"

Oliver chuckled. "I was at first, but after a while, the main thing on my mind was securing Mrs. Crabtree's reticule since she said it had a tintype of her late husband in it."

Mannerly and gallant Oliver. Even though Mrs. Crabtree criticized him and compared him to Mr. Norman, Oliver was still merciful to her. "I heard she was overjoyed when you returned it to her."

"Yes, I reckon she might think more highly of me now."

"Mrs. Vannostrand and Mrs. Hodgeson were chattering about it after super the day it happened. Apparently Mrs. Crabtree had tears in her eyes when she recounted how beholden she was to you for saving the only thing she still owned of her late husband's."

"Reckon I'm glad I could be of assistance in someone's time of need."

Genevieve's admiration for him grew. "This town is better for having you here, Oliver."

Oliver stood up straighter and color dotted his cheeks. "Thank you."

She averted her stare so as not to embarrass him further just as Reverend Harr garnered everyone's attention and read Mollie's latest newspaper article aloud. Mollie's words brought a renewed and even more profound appreciation for Oliver and his upright character.

Ellis Creek Postmaster a True Hero

Ellis Creek's very own postmaster, Oliver T. Bessell, has been proclaimed a true hero after nabbing a thief yesterday in the alley between the livery and the blacksmith. Eye witnesses say that Mr. Hansen stole Mrs. Crabtree's reticule and proceeded down the boardwalk past numerous businesses and into the alley.

"It was a most unpleasant day, and this just made it all the worse," remarked Mrs. Crabtree. "Who knew crimes such as this happened in Ellis Creek? I've lived here nearly twenty years and have never seen such audacity."

Mrs. Crabtree mentioned that the reticule was especially important to her. "Inside my reticule was not only some coins, but also the framed photo I carry around of Mr. Crabtree. It's the only tintype I have of my beloved husband. To think I could have lost it due to a thief who clearly has no conscience is unfathomable."

Oliver noticed the robbery right after it happened and took immediate action. Pedaling as fast as possible on his Overman safety bicycle, Oliver chased the thief into the alley where he seized him and held him until the sheriff could arrive.

"Mr. Bessell is a capable young man, and if he would accept it, I'd offer him a position as a deputy."

When asked if Oliver would accept the position, he said, "I'm honored by the sheriff's offer, but I am content in my role as a postmaster."

Indeed, Ellis Creek is fortunate to have Oliver as their postmaster. Mrs. Crabtree added these words in praise of Oliver. "I didn't like that young man at first. Not one bit. He was nothing like Mr. Norman and I told him as much. But after he rescued my reticule, my opinion of him dramatically changed. He and I are friends now and I consider him much like a grandson."

We in Ellis Creek are grateful for Oliver's quick thinking and levelheaded actions. As such, he will be awarded The Hero's Certificate and there will be an all-town potluck in his honor.

"Residents of Ellis Creek, it is my honor to award Oliver Bessell with The Hero's Certificate. Oliver, would you please come forward?"

Clapping ensued as Oliver walked toward Reverend Harr. Both the reverend and the sheriff shook his hand and congratulated him.

The townsfolk chattered as Oliver thanked the men for his certificate and Genevieve bustled about assisting with the potluck.

"Now that's something Mr. Norman hasn't done," said one of the townsfolk.

"Yes, he never apprehended a criminal."

"Reckon Mr. Bessell will do just fine as a postmaster."

Chapter Twelve

GENEVIEVE DISMISSED HER STUDENTS, then sat at her desk grading papers and contemplating the day's events. It was her birthday today, although no one knew except Tillie. She recalled when she was younger and her parents endeavored to create delightful birthday memories for her.

And they had.

Ma would bake her favorite cake with extra icing and Pa would do his best to act nonchalant as the day progressed. Until he came in from chores with a gift wrapped in brown paper. And while Genevieve knew exactly what to expect each year because of her parents' tradition, she was ecstatic all the same.

She missed her parents every day and perhaps even more so on holidays and birthdays. When she went to live with Aunt Blanche and Uncle Richard at the age of fourteen, her life took a distinct turn. Her relatives were overbearing, yet distant. And while they provided for her and she never went without necessities, they constantly reminded her she was not their child and could in no way compare to her snobbish cousin, Celia.

Genevieve finished grading the assignments and stood. She stretched her arms overhead and twisted at the waist to alleviate the stiffness that had settled in from bending over her desk. The door opened and Mollie bustled in, a notebook and pencil in hand. "Hello, Genevieve!"

From the moment Genevieve met Mollie, she'd liked her immediately. Gregarious and congenial, one couldn't help but like the spirited and vivacious blonde with a generous heart and the ability to speak a thousand words a minute.

"Hello, Mollie. What brings you to the schoolhouse?"

"I had the most captivating idea." Mollie waved her hands around. "I have been in desperate need of articles for the newspaper for this week's edition. Would you be amenable to being interviewed?"

Genevieve's mouth fell open. Interviewed? For the *Ellis Creek Journal*? "I'm not sure I would be a suitable candidate."

"Oh, you are more than suitable."

Genevieve wasn't sure about that. She wasn't an interesting person. Rather bland in her own mind. But the expectant expression on Mollie's face caused her to consider her friend's request. "When would you like to conduct the interview?"

"How about now?"

Genevieve had borrowed a book from Tillie and looked forward to reading it on the lawn of the boarding house when she arrived home. Perhaps she could do that another day. "All right, but I do have to warn you that it might be a short interview."

"Short is fine. I was just thinking how the townsfolk would love to know more about you."

"I should let Oliver know I won't be accompanying him to the boarding house."

A flash of concern crossed Mollie's face. "Oh, do not worry about Oliver. I informed him I would be detaining you when I paid a visit to the post office earlier today."

"Oh. All right, well thank you for telling him." How had Mollie known Genevieve would be agreeable to an interview today? Mollie wasn't usually so assuming.

Mollie perched in a pupil's desk and wrote in her oversized looping letters something across the top of the sheet of paper in the notebook. "Let's see. Where were you born?"

"In Iowa. But I only lived there until I was seven and then my family moved to Montana."

"Iowa? That is impressive."

Genevieve wasn't sure how that was impressive as many people were born in Iowa, but she didn't say as much.

"And then you moved to Fentonville."

"First we moved to Helena, and then when I was thirteen, we moved to Fentonville."

"Any brothers or sisters?"

Genevieve shook her head. "No. Just me."

Mollie proceeded to ask several questions and Genevieve answered them. For as rapidly as Mollie usually spoke, today she spoke her words with much more articulation. She also glimpsed at the clock several times.

"We could finish this tomorrow," Genevieve suggested.

"No, it's quite all right to finish it today." But just as she'd said it, Mollie again glanced at the clock before continuing with more questions.

Finally, after an hour and ten minutes, Mollie deemed the interview complete. "Thank you, Genevieve. I believe I have all I need for the article. I best be on my way." Mollie closed the notebook, tucked the pencil behind her ear, and rose to leave. "I'll see you tomorrow if not before."

A few moments later, Genevieve left the school and commenced toward the boarding house. At least there was still ample time to read after supper and assisting Mrs. Vannostrand with the chores. She stopped to inhale the heavenly scent of the rose bush on the edge of the property. Mrs. Vannostrand doted on her flowers, a gift planted by her late husband many years ago.

The boarding house was eerily quiet. Usually, young Adam would be outside tossing the ball to his dog or playing with friends in the expansive yard. Or Mrs. Vannostrand would be tending to her garden. Or Mrs. Hodgeson would be reading on the porch. Fellow boarders usually milled about the place, but not today.

Today all was silent. Even the birds, who usually sang their lovely songs from their places in the numerous trees, had hushed.

Genevieve meandered up the stairs onto the porch. The curtains were drawn. Was Mrs. Vannostrand ill? But if so, wouldn't Adam have mentioned as much at school? Usually the widow encouraged the brilliant sunlight to stream through the windows.

She turned and faced the town. Come to think about it, the town had been quiet as well. She passed only a few townsfolk on her way home, a rather unusual circumstance. And Lula's house, which she also walked by each day, was void of noise. Suspicious considering Lula's rambunctious children usually could be heard laughing and playing in the yard even before one approached Lula and Jed's house.

Genevieve tentatively turned the doorknob and pushed open the door. From the appearance of the dimly-lit room, no one was home. An aroma of something baking lingered in the air, perhaps a dessert Mrs. Vannostrand intended for after supper.

She closed the door and hastened toward the stairs, praying all was well despite the unusual circumstance.

Suddenly, out of nowhere, a cacophony of voices, excitement, and laughter filled the air. "Happy birthday!"

Genevieve stepped back and placed a hand to her heart. "Oh, my."

Several people came down the stairs, some entered from the parlor, and still others walked through the door. Genevieve would be shocked if the entire town wasn't crammed into Mrs. Vannostrand's front room.

Her students ran toward her, their bright faces shining through the dim room. Mrs. Vannostrand opened the curtains and Tillie and Lula both rushed toward her and captured her in an embrace. "Were you surprised?" Tillie asked.

"Yes…I'm…flabbergasted." Tears threatened and Genevieve blinked them away. The people of Ellis Creek had become so dear to her in such a short amount of time.

Oliver sauntered toward her, a grin on his face. "It was no easy task keeping you at the school while Tillie and Lula planned this."

"That's why we needed Mollie," added Tillie.

At just that moment, Mollie sashayed through the door. "Ma and I just closed the mercantile. Not that anyone is there anyway because they're all here." She gave Genevieve a hug. To Mrs. Vannostrand, Mollie added, "Gid will be here soon, but asks that we save him some cake."

"Cake?"

Genevieve's mouth watered at the thought. Her new friends had not only given her a surprise party, but there was cake as well? For a moment her mind reverted back to her youth and the memories of the cakes Ma would make to celebrate the momentous occasion.

"We for certain can't have a birthday party for one of Ellis Creek's favorite citizens without cake," declared Widow Jones who stood next to Mr. Norman.

Tillie's older sister, Meredith, emerged from the kitchen with a cake topped with plentiful icing and several candles. Everyone offered their congratulations for her special day.

And Genevieve thanked the Lord for leading her to Ellis Creek.

Oliver watched as Genevieve unfolded the homemade cards from each of her pupils. It had been worth all of Tillie and Lula's planning to make this a special day for Genevieve. She was exceptionally pretty today with her purple shirt and brown skirt.

Oliver chuckled to himself. If his youngest sister were here, she'd refer to Genevieve's shirt color as plum, rather than purple. His sister prided herself on being precise.

Genevieve's eyes sparkled as they caught his glance, and for a brief moment, Oliver forgot to breathe. Perhaps someday, if it was the Lord's will, he would capture the heart of the woman who was beginning to mean a lot to him.

He hoped Genevieve liked the present he'd prepared for her. Catching Tillie's eye, he nodded and proceeded to discreetly leave the house without Genevieve noticing.

He retrieved the ladder, the prepared rectangle-shaped piece of wood, and some sturdy rope from the barn behind the boarding house. Checking to be sure Genevieve was still inside, he wandered toward the towering oak tree and placed the wood piece on the ground. He carefully propped the ladder against the tree and, rope in hand, climbed to the second-to-the-top rung. Oliver looped the rope over the strongest branch and attached the piece of wood.

Five minutes later, Tillie led Genevieve, eyes closed, out the door and slowly to the oak tree.

"You can open your eyes," Tillie announced.

Genevieve's eyes fluttered open. She pivoted her gaze from the swing to him, then back to the swing again. "Is this for me?"

"It is," he answered.

"Oh!" Genevieve clasped her hands together. "Thank you."

"Why don't you sit on it for a spell?" Widow Jones said.

Genevieve gingerly took a step toward the swing and sat and wrapped her hands around the ropes. Oliver gave her a gentle push. "We know you like to sit and read your books after school, so we thought…" Oliver cleared his throat. "We thought you might like a swing instead of always sitting on the bench."

He stood beside her then and noticed she had closed her eyes as the breeze blew back the wisps of hair that had escaped from her braid. Had he ever known anyone as lovely as Genevieve? And not just her appearance, for Pa would remind him a woman of fine character was far more than that.

And indeed, Genevieve was smart, considerate, gentle, and kind.

"Don't you think, Oliver?"

Mrs. Hodson's words brought Oliver from his thoughts of Genevieve back to the situation at hand. "Pardon me?"

"I was just saying your decision to make Genevieve a swing was a remarkable idea, don't you think, Oliver?"

Genevieve's eye caught his. "I love the swing. Thank you so much."

"Did you used to be a carpenter, Mr. Bessell?" Little Gabe asked, peering up at him.

"My pa built a lot of things and he taught me how to craft things as well." Oliver thought of the countless hours he'd spent with Pa learning how to build everything from a cradle for his baby nephew to a neighbor's home.

Mr. Norman clapped a hand on his shoulder. "Well done," he said.

The children ran to play a game of tag and the adults convened by the porch where Mrs. Vannostrand offered lemonade.

"I really appreciate this, Oliver," Genevieve said, showing no signs of relinquishing the swing anytime soon. "It reminds me of one my pa made for me when I was a little girl." Joy shone in her smile.

"I'm glad you like it."

"And the birthday party too. Thank you."

Oliver kicked at a pebble in the dirt. "You can thank Tillie and Lula for planning it."

She smiled at him again and it did something to Oliver's insides he couldn't quite explain, for he'd never been in love before.

Until he'd met Genevieve Amsel.

Chapter Thirteen

AT CHURCH THAT SUNDAY, Widow Jones leaned toward Genevieve and spoke in a slightly-quieter tone than usual. "That Oliver is such a nice young man, don't you think, Genevieve?"

The family in the pew two rows in front of them turned to peer at the commotion behind them. If Widow Jones was attempting to whisper, she was failing miserably.

"Yes, he is."

Genevieve peered behind them to reassure herself that Oliver was nowhere in their vicinity. Thankfully he hadn't yet arrived for Sunday service and had left the boarding house after Genevieve, Mrs. Vannostrand, and Adam.

"Indeed, such a nice young man, that Oliver Bessell." Widow Jones repeated, a beaming smile on her face as if proud of herself for acknowledging Oliver's character. She patted Genevieve's arm. "And don't you think, dear, that he would be a fine man to court?"

If Irving hadn't broken her heart into a million pieces, causing Genevieve to fear ever falling in love again, then yes, Oliver might be a suitable man for courtship. But as it was, Genevieve had made a promise with herself to never fall in love again. No more tears that way. And since she always exercised caution, prudence, and extreme deliberation before making any decision, she upheld all, if not most, of those choices.

In the case of Oliver...she heard his voice and she glanced over her shoulder to see he'd just entered the church. She allowed her gaze to linger on him for the briefest of moments. He chatted amiably with Mrs. Hodgeson, who, with her husband, had also entered. Something the older woman said caused him to chuckle.

And yes, Oliver did have a nice laugh.

And a kind heart. She'd seen that first hand when he assisted the cantankerous Mrs. Crabtree the time she nearly lost her balance while walking. Then the time he recovered her reticule for her. Courageous also described Oliver.

And Oliver was a godly man who loved Jesus. Genevieve knew he studied God's Word and did his best to abide by it.

And he did love his family, which was important. He spoke of them frequently and how much he missed them.

And he was smart and worked hard at the post office.

And Oliver was a good and loyal friend with whom she'd shared some things she'd never before shared with anyone except Tillie.

And when he wore his spectacles while reading something, at times they'd slide down his nose and he'd gingerly right them with an index finger and a quirky shrug specific only to him.

And other times he'd forget he'd pushed them to the top of his head and would set about looking for them while Genevieve attempted not to giggle.

And he was handsome.

Oh, yes, Oliver Bessell was quite handsome with his dark ruffled hair, soft green eyes full of compassion, strong broad shoulders and lean stature.

But no, she couldn't—wouldn't—allow herself to fall in love with him for fear of being hurt again. What if she did give him her heart and he decided she wasn't the one for him, just as Irving had?

"Don't you think?" Widow Jones was asking.

"Begging your pardon, Widow Jones? I apologize but I didn't hear you."

"No, I don't imagine you did, what with your focus on a certain young gentleman." Widow Jones raised a brow and smirked, a twinkle in her faded eyes.

"Oh! I..." Genevieve's face suddenly warmed and she fiddled with one of the tortoiseshell combs in her hair.

Widow Jones nodded. "That's what I thought. You're fonder of Oliver than you care to admit."

Genevieve opened her mouth to dispute Widow Jones's insinuation, but no words came out. She swallowed and tried again. "While I do find Oliver to be a charming young man, I'm not interested in courtship, not now or ever, for that matter."

"Not interested in courtship? Not now and not ever? Whyever not? If I may ask."

"As you may know, my heart was broken when my fiancé, Irving, decided to cancel our wedding just two weeks before we were to exchange our nuptials."

Widow Jones closed her eyes and held a hand to her bosom. "Yes, I do recall hearing about that discourteous man who broke your heart. But, Genevieve, if I may offer some advice, not every man is like Irving. And clearly he wasn't the one for you."

Her words struck something deep inside Genevieve's thoughts and she played the words over and over again intermittently throughout the church service.

And when Oliver took his place beside her as he always did, her stomach fluttered, and even more so when his arm brushed against hers.

Could she remain true to her promise?

The odds were not in her favor.

Oliver hoisted a crate of goods into the mercantile then returned to the wagon for an additional load. On days when the post office lacked customers or Oliver was temporarily finished with his duties, he would assist Gideon with unloading freight.

While Oliver considered himself strong and capable, Gid was a mountain of a man with extraordinary strength. He lifted twice what Oliver could and made half the trips to and from the wagon.

"Sure appreciate your help," Gid said when they'd finished. "How about some meatloaf and lemonade from the restaurant?"

Oliver never refused a noonday meal or lemonade, and the boarding house only served breakfast and supper. A meal at the restaurant was far more appetizing than the two sandwiches Oliver brought in his tin pail. He propped a handwritten sign in the post office window indicating he'd be back soon and joined Gid for a walk to Ellis Creek's new restaurant.

The waitress seated them by the window where they could watch passersby. While they awaited their food, they discussed deliveries, Gid's most recent trip to Fentonville, cattle prices, how the mill had brought an influx of folks to Ellis Creek, and finally, Genevieve's birthday party last week.

"Seems Genevieve enjoyed her surprise birthday party," Gid said, taking a drink of his lemonade.

"I think it meant a lot to her with being away from home and all."

Gid smirked. "Any chance you might fancy her?"

The question caught Oliver unawares and he nearly choked on his lemonade. "Genevieve?"

"Yes, you know, the woman you spend a lot of time with. The one you made a swing for?"

"I know who Genevieve is, I just...uh..."

Thankfully Gid wasn't really listening to Oliver's bumbling words as he was gaping out the window. Oliver followed the direction of Gid's gaze. Mollie walked down the boardwalk with her mother, and Gid eagerly waved as they passed the restaurant. Mollie saw him and waved back. She then paused for a moment and the two of them smiled at each other through the window.

"Really, Gid, you could go outside and have a conversation with Mollie. I'll still be here when you return."

"Uh..." But Gid didn't remove his gaze nor did he stop waving at Mollie. "Uh, no, we'll be talking later when I go to her parents' house for supper."

"And didn't you just talk with her when we were delivering the supplies?"

"There was a customer part of that time."

If Oliver didn't know better, he'd think Gid and Mollie were ready for courtship rather than just friendship. "Speaking of fancying someone..."

"Nah, Mollie and I are best friends."

Just the words Oliver predicted Gid would say.

"But you, on the other hand, I think you do fancy Genevieve."

Oliver removed his pocket watch and stared at it longer than necessary. "Genevieve, you say?"

"Yes, Genevieve. The new school teacher. Your friend. The one you made the swing for. The one you sit with at church. The one you walk home with each day."

Gid's ornery snicker told Oliver he'd not get away with masking his thoughts about Genevieve, not in Gideon's presence, anyhow.

"She's a nice woman and pretty too. She's smart and loves the Lord and has a nice sense of humor. And she's nice to others..."

"And you've used the word 'nice' three times in two seconds. Not a customary thing for Postmaster Bessell."

Heat flooded Oliver's face. When had Genevieve come to mean more to him than just a friend? He couldn't pinpoint the exact day, but it *had* happened. And it wasn't all that recent. He thought of the letter he wrote her that he tucked safely on the top of his bureau at the boarding house. This morning he'd pilfered through the growing stack of disorganization—also known as his belongings—to re-read Lorelei's letter about how to capture Genevieve's heart.

Now that he gave it further consideration, Oliver hadn't recalled seeing the letter to Genevieve.

A distressing thought entered his mind. Could he have misplaced it?

Gid, always the chatty sort, continued speaking. "Genevieve told Mollie and Mollie told me that Genevieve will never fall in love again after, as Mollie put it, 'that scoundrel in Fentonville decided to cancel their wedding.'"

"She said she'd never fall in love again?" Why did it feel like heartburn was settling into Oliver's chest although he'd not yet eaten?

"Not taking the chance on love ever again, according to Mollie."

Of course, Mollie did have a tendency to gossip. "Mollie could be incorrect."

"Could be, but probably not. Good thing you don't fancy Genevieve."

Oliver averted his gaze from Gideon to the other customers so his friend couldn't see what could be an indicator of Oliver's true feelings. As he'd been reminded countless times by his sisters, everything he was thinking about was written all over his face.

If Mollie's words were correct and Genevieve planned never to fall in love again, how could Oliver convince her to change her mind?

Chapter Fourteen

GENEVIEVE SAT ON THE bench outside the boarding house after school. Little Gabe and Adam played in the yard with Adam's dog. Mr. and Mrs. Hodgeson sat on the porch and drank lemonade, and Mrs. Vannostrand tended to her gardens.

Just as Genevieve was about to begin reading her book, she noticed Oliver returning home from a day at the post office. They hadn't been able to walk home together today and she missed his company.

She closed the book and placed it in her lap. Talking with Oliver was preferable even to the best book.

Oliver slowed his pace as he neared her. "Hello, Genevieve."

"Hello, Oliver. Did you have a good day at the post office?"

"I did. How was school?"

"The students did a splendid job on their writing assignments. I could not have been more pleased. And our new pupils have come so far in their orthography. As a matter of fact, we're preparing for another spelling bee."

Oliver grinned at her and Genevieve was reminded what a pleasant smile he had.

"Would you care to sit?" She gestured at the seat beside her. Ever since she and Oliver had become friends, she anticipated their daily stroll from work so they could visit about their day. And each morning, Genevieve eagerly awaited seeing him at the breakfast table and receiving his delightful notes, short as they were. She noticed the envelope in his hand. "Delivering mail today?" she asked.

"Actually, this one is for me. It's from my ma."

"Have you read it yet?"

"I have." Oliver traced the penmanship on the envelope with his finger.

Genevieve didn't wish to sound nosy, but she was curious. "And is all well?"

"It is. But I miss my family."

She admired Oliver's closeness with his family. "Are you considering moving back to Bozeman?" Genevieve held her breath as she awaited his answer, realizing that if he moved, she would miss him.

Oliver rubbed the back of his neck. "No, I'd like to stay in Ellis Creek. I like my job, the people, and the church."

Relief flooded her. Friends such as Oliver Bessell did not enter one's life on a regular basis. He, Tillie, Lula, and Mollie had all become so dear to her in the short time she'd resided in Ellis Creek.

Oliver retrieved the letter from the envelope and unfolded it. Mrs. Bessell had lovely penmanship, her letters flowing elegantly across the page, not too large and not too small. He turned the paper over to reveal more of the letter on the backside. "As you can see, my mother enjoys writing."

"I can honestly say there is nothing wrong with that."

Oliver chuckled at her pronouncement. "She would tend to agree with you. And she's an intelligent woman who shared that knowledge with my sisters and me. Before we attended school in Bozeman, we lived on the far corner of the ranch and Ma schooled us each day. I think that's why I have such a love for learning."

Genevieve shared his love for learning. "That's one thing I adore about teaching. I learn once again alongside the children. Does your ma write often?"

"Yes, about every couple of weeks or so." He glanced at the letter and cleared his throat. "These words are the best words of the entire letter. 'Your pa and I are thrilled to tell you that we will soon be moving to Fentonville. A friend of your father's mentioned there was a ranch foreman position available there and since the current owner of the ranch in Bozeman is planning to sell, we anticipate moving to Fentonville this fall.'" Oliver's eyes brightened and a broad grin covered his entire face. "I've missed them and this will make it easier to visit since they'll be much closer to Ellis Creek."

"That's wonderful! Will your sisters be moving to Fentonville as well?"

"My oldest sister, yes, but I'm not sure about my second-oldest. Her husband is a banker in Bozeman. My two youngest sisters still reside with our parents, so they'll be moving with them as well. I've spoken to Lorelei, my second-to-the-youngest sister, a time or two about possibly moving to Ellis Creek."

"I'm so happy for you."

Oliver folded the letter and placed it back in its envelope. "Do you ever consider moving from Ellis Creek?"

"No, this is my home now."

"Do you always see yourself teaching school?"

Genevieve had grown accustomed to the numerous questions they often asked each other and figured she knew more about Oliver and contrariwise than she knew about many other friends.

His fingers brushed hers and a jolt of something zipped up her arm.

"No, I mean, yes, I do always see myself teaching school as long as the Lord allows, anyhow."

Oliver's fingers remained by hers and she wondered what it might be like for him to hold her hand. At the thought, heat crept up her face.

Remember, Genevieve, what Irving did.

Yes, but this is not Irving. This is Oliver.

True, but what if Oliver is like Irving?

He's not.

How can you be so sure?

"Genevieve?"

She extracted herself from the internal conversation. If Oliver knew she argued with herself, he'd think her a featherbrain.

"Yes?"

They sat staring at each other, Genevieve waiting for Oliver to elaborate and Oliver with an indiscernible expression on his face.

"Genevieve…" he repeated, his voice hoarse.

"Yes?"

Her mind conjured up a million things he could say to her. Would he tell her he cared for her as more than a friend? That he wished to court her?

But you were just saying you'd never fall in love again because of Irving.

Yes, but I do feel differently for Oliver than I ever felt for Irving. And…

"I…," Oliver began.

The moment was broken by Mrs. Vannostrand ringing the bell for supper.

Oliver cleared his throat. "Reckon we should go inside for supper."

And Genevieve knew she would wonder for the rest of the evening what Oliver truly meant to say.

One, or all, of his sisters would term him a dullard or a simpleton for not being able to find his words when speaking with Genevieve.

But how could he declare his affection for her if he didn't know if she would accept it?

What if she informed him she would never court someone like him?

He'd taken to heart Lorelei's advice and had spent time with Genevieve so she could know what kind of man he was. Oliver had performed kind gestures, such as partaking in the arrangements for her birthday party and building her the swing.

Oliver *hadn't* been able to write the more detailed letters Tillie and Lula requested, however. Well, except for one.

One that he still needed to locate beneath the pile of items on his bureau.

He lingered outside for a few more minutes pondering his absentmindedness. Finally, so as not to be late for supper, he entered the boarding house and headed toward the table.

"Oliver?"

Mrs. Crabtree limped toward him.

Ever since he'd rescued her reticule, Mrs. Crabtree's contempt toward him had changed, and she even took it upon herself to call him by his first name.

"Hello, Mrs. Crabtree."

"You know how you are always leaving those little notes for Genevieve?"

A sick feeling pitted in his stomach. "Yes?"

Mrs. Crabtree lifted her wrinkled chin. "Well, it just so happened that Adam brought me one of those letters today. Apparently he found it in his notebook, but you weren't home yet, so he gave it to me. The young boy was worried about it being important." A glint shone in her eyes. "He mentioned something about stopping by and interviewing you about your occupation. The note must have gotten scooped up by accident."

The sick feeling intensified. Hopefully it was just a short note that Adam brought to Mrs. Crabtree and not *the* letter. "Yes, he did have more questions about being a postmaster." Oliver recalled Adam setting his notebook on the bureau to take notes. He also recalled being impressed that someone so young could spell so well. But Oliver never fathomed he'd have to be worried about the letter to Genevieve disappearing into Adam's notebook.

"Now, mind you," Mrs. Crabtree continued, "I did not open it to read it, but I did put it at Genevieve's place setting for you this evening."

Oliver's mouth fell open, but no words came out. *Lord, please don't let it be* the *letter detailing my feelings for her.*

"No need to thank me. Yes, I know I should have waited until breakfast since that's when you always give her the notes, but perhaps she'd like a note at suppertime as well. And since you were such a hero, I figured it was the least I could do to return the favor. I know she'll appreciate it just as much as your other letters."

Mrs. Crabtree ambled off, but Oliver's feet were stuck in place. If Genevieve opened the note and read of his feelings for her...

Lord, I come to You and ask—no, beg—for Your assistance. Please don't let Genevieve have already read the letter.

Unfortunately, he wouldn't have time to check the top of his bureau to alleviate his concerns about which note Adam had given to Mrs. Crabtree.

Oliver crept around the corner and into the dining area. Genevieve sat in the chair across the table from him and in her hands was an unfolded piece of paper.

His sisters would chastise him for being dramatic when he lifted his next prayer, but he meant it in all seriousness.

Lord, if I die here today because of embarrassment, please see to it that my family is well taken care of, especially Ma since she'll be heartbroken to have lost her only son.

Genevieve was surprised to have discovered a note at the supper table. Usually Oliver left his cheerful notes during breakfast. She unfolded it and was flabbergasted when she noticed the number of words on the page and wondered if perhaps an imposter had written it. But when she squinted to read the miniscule penmanship, she knew for certain it was Oliver's.

Dear Genevieve,

I believe I am falling in love with you. Each evening after we part ways, I find that I can't wait until the following day to spend time with you again. Our talks, walks, and time spent together have further anchored my feelings for you. I know Irving hurt you when he decided not to marry you. He was a fool to make that decision. You have my word that I would never hurt you and if given the chance, would love you forever.

You have a strong faith and your love for Jesus is apparent. You are a patient teacher with your pupils and a compassionate woman. I appreciate your grace toward Mrs. Crabtree, which isn't an easy feat.

I have grown fond of your smile and the way your blue eyes light up when you are happy about something. I like your laugh and your wit. I've never met a prettier woman than you.

I hope to someday have a chance to win your affections.

Yours truly,

She inhaled a deep breath. Delight billowed in her heart even as flames of heat burned her cheeks.

Oliver hoped to someday have a chance to win her affections?

He promised never to hurt her?

But to love her forever?

Genevieve heard the voices of her fellow boarders, but her attention was focused solely on Oliver's letter. She read it again.

And a third time.

Then she raised her eyes above the letter and noticed Oliver standing near the edge of the table as if frozen to the spot. His eyes widened and his mouth moved, but there was no audible sound.

The poor, sweet man appeared horrified.

But why if he meant to leave the letter for her?

"There now, Oliver, come have a seat at the table," Mrs. Crabtree admonished. "Genevieve has read your note. From all appearances, she's read it more than once."

The room was silent with the exception of Mrs. Crabtree tapping her gnarled fingers on the table and Mr. Hodgeson's nasally breathing.

"I...uh..."

"Oliver?" Genevieve's voice sounded tinny in her own ears.

Their eyes connected and he nodded slowly.

"You have."

"I...I have?"

"You have won my affections."

"I have..." A smile lit his handsome face and he stood up straighter. "I have won your affections?"

Mrs. Hodgeson inclined toward her husband. "There now, isn't this just the sweetest thing? Remember when you won my affections?"

"Reckon I still have them," he said and tossed an adoring glance at his bride.

"Genevieve?" Oliver asked, walking toward her.

"Yes, Oliver?"

"Would you do me the honor of courting me?"

"Yes, Oliver, I will."

There was clapping all around and Mrs. Crabtree muttered, "It's about time he asked her."

But Genevieve was oblivious to it all.

For her thoughts were on the humble man of whom she'd grown fond.

Chapter Fifteen

OLIVER CLASPED HIS HANDS behind his head and stared at the ceiling. Was it really true that Genevieve accepted his proposal of courtship at supper tonight? Was it really true he'd survived the awkwardness of standing near the table watching Genevieve read a letter she was never meant to read?

He blew out a deep breath and thanked the Lord again for small miracles.

It would be a restless night, but not for the usual reasons nights were restless. Instead, it was because the woman he'd grown fond of in a few short months had agreed to be a bigger part of his life.

Please, Lord, let me be a worthy husband to her someday.

Oliver swung his legs over the side of the bed, lit the lantern, and pulled a sheet of stationery from the haphazard pile on his bureau. Ma, Pa, and his sisters ought to know he'd found the woman God had planned for him. It was a certainty that Ma would pass the letter on to his older sisters once everyone else had read it, and for that he was grateful. No sense in writing several letters that shared the same information.

Dear Ma, Pa, and Sisters,

This evening, I asked a woman named Genevieve Amsel to court me. She accepted. I hope you can meet her once you move to Fentonville. She's a godly woman who teaches at the school here. I think you will all like her. She is sweet and kind and has a nice personality. And because I know my youngest sister will ask, yes, Genevieve is beautiful.

Lorelei, thank you for the advice you recently gave me. I hope sometime you can visit Ellis Creek and see the new library here that Tillie Fairbanks is hoping to open someday.

Hope you are faring well and preparing for your move. I plan to travel to Fentonville when you arrive to help you get settled.

Miss you all.

Sincerely,

Your Favorite Son and Favorite Brother

Genevieve ruminated over Oliver's letter deep into the night. After she'd re-read it fourteen times.

How could she have ever thought he was anything like Irving?

Her only regret was that Pa was not here to walk her down the aisle when, in future months, Oliver proposed. And Uncle Richard likely would not care to do so. Nor would he care to be asked for her hand in marriage. Unless it was by Irving.

A bittersweet lump formed in her throat, but she quickly shoved aside any dismal thoughts. Tomorrow couldn't arrive soon enough so she could share the news with Tillie.

The following day after school, Genevieve joined Tillie, Lula, and Mollie on Lula's front porch for lemonade. "I could not wait to tell you all—Oliver asked me to court him!"

Tillie and Lula shared a knowing glance and chorused an exuberant, "Congratulations!"

Even Baby Jed let out a squeal of delight and clapped his pudgy hands.

Mollie gave her a hug. "That is thrilling. And to think, you two started out as the best of friends."

Lula popped a jawbreaker in her mouth. "Sometimes the best of friends can become husband and wife. Maybe that's what will happen with you and Gid."

Mollie shook her head so swiftly her blonde curls bounced. "No, not Gid and me."

"Don't be so sure," added Tillie.

"Oh, I'm sure," declared Mollie. "We are only best friends."

Tillie and Lula gave each other a conspiring nudge at Mollie's response. Tillie then rested her hand on Genevieve's arm. "We are so happy for you. Oliver is a kind man and so smart too. And he's a hero."

Genevieve's cheeks prickled with heat. "That he is."

"Do tell how he asked you. Was it while the two of you were sitting on the bench? Or was it when he was pushing you in the swing he made for you? Or perhaps during a walk home? Or maybe while the two of you spent time in the boarding house parlor after supper? Or during a walk to church?" Tillie clasped her hands together. "Do tell us *all* the details."

Genevieve proceeded to apprise her friends about the letter. "I was so sure I would never fall in love again, but I see now that God had better plans. Much better."

"You two do make a handsome couple," Tillie declared. "And the poor Ellis Creek school board. It seems they must find a new teacher on a regular basis."

"Indeed," agreed Mollie. "First Tillie and now Genevieve."

"And after your courtship and Oliver asks you to marry him, then three of the four of us will be married women. All except one." Lula jutted her chin toward Mollie and continued with her playful hints. "Yes, only one will be unmarried, but perhaps she will fall in love with a handsome gent from the mill. Or maybe Widow Jones has a long-lost relative she could arrange to court you. Or…"

Tillie shrugged. "Or, she could just fall in love with Gid."

"You don't just fall in love with someone, silly," said Mollie. "Gid and I will never court for that would ruin our friendship. But I do have some other interesting news I thought I'd share since we're discussing true love."

"Oh?" asked Genevieve. "Could it be you are speaking of Widow Jones and Mr. Norman? I do believe Widow Jones is quite fond of Mr. Norman and apparently has been baking goodies for him. Oliver also said that Mr. Norman's face turned bright red when he discussed how 'purdy' Widow Jones was during their time fishing at the creek."

"Those two are so endearing. Perhaps Genevieve and Oliver could have their wedding at the same time as Widow Jones and Mr. Norman," suggested Tillie.

"Well, you better add one more couple to that wedding." Mollie leaned forward, her eyes growing large as they always did when she had special information to share. "I first became suspicious when Leopold Arkwright from the bank came into the mercantile to purchase several bags of jawbreakers in a brief amount of time. Of course, we all knew that Collette had set her cap for him from the second she entered the bank that day. According to sources who choose to remain nameless, Leopold and Collette are courting. And while she has since returned to Helena, I heard that Leopold has plans to visit there soon."

Mollie's exaggerated tone caused a round of laughter among the friends.

And a thought passed through Genevieve's mind. If Irving hadn't decided to cancel their engagement and subsequent wedding, she would never have found Oliver, her group of friends, or the welcoming town of Ellis Creek.

Chapter Sixteen

OLIVER OPENED THE CANVAS mailbag and unloaded the letters, just as he always did when Gid delivered it from Fentonville. Today there were only six letters, and he distributed five of them into their proper slots. The last letter, however, was unreadable.

He pushed his glasses further on his nose and squinted in an attempt to read the smeared penmanship. The only legible words were "Ellis Creek, Montana," written in slanted writing toward the lower portion of the envelope.

Oliver removed his magnifying lens from the drawer in his desk. He held it above the blurred string of words. Was that a "B" or a "D" on the first line?

Upon closer examination, the envelope had been a casualty of some sort of moisture. Had it been left in the rain? Had it fallen in a puddle? Had someone spilled something on it and that's what blurred the ink?

Oliver set about completing his other work duties. Perhaps Genevieve could read the writing on the envelope and determine to whom it belonged. He pulled out his pocket watch—only three more hours until he would see her again. Ever since he'd proposed courtship last week, they'd spent nearly every possible moment together, especially in the evenings when they met in the parlor under Mrs. Crabtree's watchful eye.

Finally, after finishing his duties, tending to the needs of four customers, and ensuring everything was ready for tomorrow, Oliver met Genevieve at the schoolhouse. He offered his elbow, and she placed her hand through the crook of his arm. "You are prettier than ever today, Genevieve," he said, noting her bright smile.

They perched on the bench outside the boarding house and Oliver withdrew the envelope. "I can only ascertain what the last line of wording is. Even the return address is smeared and illegible." He slid closer to Genevieve so they could both examine it.

"I can't see anything but maybe a "B" or a "D" on that top line," she said.

"That's what I thought too. I guess we could write down a list of townsfolk who have a "B" or a "D" in their name, presumably at the beginning of their name."

"That will be extremely cumbersome, especially since Ellis Creek has grown so much as of late."

Genevieve was correct. But what else could they do?

A mild breeze blew and Oliver caught a whiff of a pleasing flowery scent. He removed his spectacles and placed them on the bench beside him, then turned his head slightly and met Genevieve's gaze. He reached up and tenderly stroked her cheek.

"Genevieve?"

"Yes?"

"May I kiss you?"

"Yes," she whispered.

Had he not been so close to her and listening intently for her answer, Oliver would have missed it.

A quick perusal indicated the children playing in a nearby tree, Mrs. Hodgeson engrossed in a book on the porch, and no one paying any attention to them.

Oliver gently took her face in his hands as their lips met.

Genevieve's heart fluttered and tendrils of anticipation whirled through her belly. She allowed her mind to dream of someday being married to Oliver and sharing plentiful kisses.

When he pulled away a few seconds later, they sat, staring into each other's eyes. Would Oliver kiss her again?

"Well, hello, you two."

Widow Jones's buoyant chatter interrupted Genevieve's thoughts. "Hello, Widow Jones. What brings you to the boarding house?"

The elderly woman leaned on her cane. "Mr. Norman brought me into town today for some social time with friends and a visit to the mercantile."

Oliver quirked an eyebrow and Genevieve could almost hear the rumble of a chuckle. "Mr. Norman brought you to town?" he asked.

"Oh, yes. He's such a charitable gentleman."

Was that a crimson glow covering Widow Jones's precious face? She averted her gaze toward the children playing hide and seek. "Oh, to be young again..." She exhaled a wistful sigh. "I've come to visit Mrs. Hodgeson. At Tillie's suggestion, we've started a book society of sorts. We both read the same book and then we discuss it. How are you two faring today?"

"We are attempting to unriddle the mystery of a letter. The address was somehow faded, likely due to the envelope sustaining moisture," said Genevieve.

"May I see the envelope?"

Oliver handed it to her. "Would you care to have a seat, Widow?"

"Certainly." She crowded between Genevieve and Oliver and scrutinized the envelope. "When my grand-children were young'uns, a schoolbook fell into the creek. You can imagine my distress because I didn't have the funds to replace it. The words on the page faded and blurred, but I became adept at determining what they were and wrote the letters over the nearly unreadable words. Therefore, I learned how to decipher words that had nearly disappeared." She squinted at the envelope, held it at arm's length, then held it close again. She rotated it until it was upside-down, then returned it to its upright position. "I do believe I see a 'B' on this. Yes, a name that begins with a 'B'."

"And not a 'D'?" Oliver asked.

Widow Jones's brow knitted. "No, it's a 'B'. Now let me see if I can solve the mystery of any other letters." She studied the envelope for a few more seconds. "There is an 'er' at the end and then no other letters on that line from what I can ascertain."

Oliver stroked his beardless chin. "A name beginning with a 'B' and ending with an 'er'...that's it! Mr. Bellinger."

"Yes, yes, that could very well be the case," agreed Widow Jones. "And if it is a letter to Mr. Bellinger, you ought to deliver it to him posthaste. I know he's been worrying something dreadful about his daughter because he has not heard from her in some time. How the envelope came to be in such a dismal state is beyond me, but I do believe, given my ability to decipher, that the addressee's name is 'Bellinger'."

Genevieve thought of the disagreeable man who lived several miles from Ellis Creek. "It's likely this letter took longer than necessary to arrive here due to its condition. Poor man. He must be consumed with worry."

"I know I would be. Now, why don't you two take this letter to him tomorrow morning? It's Saturday so there will be no need to attend school or work at the post office. I shall accompany you as your chaperone." Widow Jones's lifted chin and erect posture indicated she'd have no arguments.

"If you're sure, Widow," said Oliver.

"Of course I'm sure. I'll see you both at seven o'clock tomorrow morning. Have Mrs. Vannostrand pack us all a noonday meal and I will provide the cookies."

Genevieve and Oliver retrieved Widow Jones at promptly seven o'clock in the wagon Oliver had borrowed from Jed. When Oliver assisted Genevieve into the wagon, her heart did a somersault, and she was reminded all over again about the kiss they shared yesterday.

Widow Jones was sandwiched between them, and a few moments later, Oliver beckoned the horses toward Mr. Bellinger's house.

Genevieve appreciated the Montana summers. Warm, pleasant, and low in humidity. She marveled at the plush green fields and the mountains in the distance, some of which boasted snow on their tallest peaks.

"Now, you two just go about your conversation and don't mind me. I aim to read the entire way there." Widow Jones held the book steady in her lap, her arthritic fingers curled around the edges of it. She would read for a few seconds, then continue chattering about everything from the weather to her grandchildren, to the fact she would soon be a great-grandma, and how she and Mr. Norman discovered they had much in common.

Genevieve and Oliver traded a glance, and his eyes flickered with amusement as he grinned at her over the top of Widow Jones's head.

He was a dapper man to be sure, with his dark ruffled hair the color of chocolate, and his warm green eyes. Genevieve appreciated his faith, his intelligence, and his good-natured and easygoing temperament.

Absolutely nothing like Irving.

Widow Jones finally focused on reading, her mouth moving in silent tandem as she did so. Such a dear and precious woman.

Genevieve and Oliver's lively and plentiful conversations caused the time to pass quickly and after an hour, they arrived at Mr. Bellinger's cabin.

Oliver was somewhat apprehensive about talking with Mr. Bellinger. After all, the man hadn't taken too kindly to him replacing Mr. Norman.

And what if Widow Jones was incorrect about to whom the letter belonged?

The widow prattled on during the duration of their journey intermittently between reading, but Oliver's attention was on the beautiful blonde woman who sat on the other side of Widow Jones. Never would he have imagined he'd be grateful for Mrs. Crabtree's hasty behavior in giving the letter to Genevieve.

When they reached the Bellinger home, the owner greeted them, his bowlegged gait slow and somewhat unsteady. "What are you folks doing here? Mr. Norman would never arrive unannounced. Young man, you're what some would call presumptuous."

Oliver attempted to push aside the man's words. "Mr. Bellinger, we've come to deliver a letter to you."

Mr. Bellinger firmed his mouth in a stern line. "All right. Nothing I can do then but invite you inside and take a gander at what you've come to deliver." Mr. Bellinger shuffled toward the house and gestured to them to take a seat at the worn walnut table.

Shouldn't Mr. Bellinger be more eager to see if the letter was from his daughter? Oliver pulled out the chairs for Widow Jones and Genevieve, then took a seat beside Mr. Bellinger.

"Who do you reckon it's from?" Mr. Bellinger asked, caution radiating from his narrowed eyes.

"We're not sure, sir. The address is mostly gone on the front. Seems the envelope met with a puddle or perhaps a rainstorm on its way to its destination."

"Then how do you know it's for me?"

Oliver tamped down the realization that Mr. Bellinger could be correct. "We are hoping it is."

"Yes, and as a professional decipherer..." began Widow Jones, "As one who prides herself in being able to read words smudged by water, I believe with some accuracy that this letter does belong to you."

At the widow's proclamation, Mr. Bellinger eased a bit, his shoulders relaxing as he settled into his chair. "Don't want to be disappointed if this isn't what I hope it to be."

Another morsel of Ma's wisdom entered Oliver's mind. *"We never know what pain someone is enduring at present. That's why we should always model the compassion of our Savior. He cared deeply for others, as should we."*

Oliver prayed he would have compassion for the man beside him.

Mr. Bellinger slit open the envelope with his pocketknife and withdrew the letter. His hands shook as he unfolded it. "Some of it is unreadable," he said. "But..."

A single tear traveled down his leathery face. "It's from her."

Oliver traded glances with Genevieve. Sympathy radiated from her countenance.

Mr. Bellinger wiped his face with the back of his hand and his gravelly voice shook as he spoke. "Thought I done lost her when I hadn't heard nothing for months. But she's fine and well. A praise to the Lord for that." He smoothed the letter against the table, his head bent over to re-read the words. "Says here she and her husband had been ill for some time. Can't read the next couple of sentences since they are smudged, but then it says she's fine now and hopes to hear from me soon." His voice broke. "Can you wait a few minutes while I write a return letter?"

Before he could stop himself, Oliver clamped a reassuring grip on the man's shoulder. "We can do that, sir. Take all the time you need."

"And in the meantime, I'll serve us all a noonday meal." Widow Jones scooted back her chair. "Mr. Bellinger, I have brought cookies so I do hope you'll help yourself and we can leave some behind for you for another day."

Genevieve rose from the table as well. "I'll assist you, Widow."

Mr. Bellinger turned toward Oliver. "Thank you. Mr. Norman would never have done this."

"Sir, I am not Mr. Norman, but I do aim to try my best to do everything as if for the Lord, and that includes working as a postmaster."

"Wasn't quite finished with my words yet. You see, Mr. Norman would never have done this. He was an outstanding postmaster, but he wouldn't have traveled all this way to deliver a letter he wasn't even sure was for me. I'm much obliged, Postmaster Bessell, for what you've done."

Epilogue

Genevieve settled into the buggy Oliver borrowed from Jed's livery. Aunt Blanche and Uncle Richard had not attended the wedding, causing Genevieve a mixture of relief and disappointment. But Oliver's family arrived and welcomed her into their lives.

And now Oliver's horses clip-clopped down the road toward the house at the edge of town that was now theirs. Excitement trilled through her at the thought of a new life with Oliver. Sweet, kind, and handsome Oliver. The one who'd won her heart when she'd vehemently promised never to fall in love again.

She marveled at how the entire town celebrated their nuptials with them. Tillie's sister, Meredith, had sewn

Genevieve's dress. The exquisite gown with leg-o-mutton sleeves, a cameo button at the high neckline, and lace ruffles on the bodice surpassed any wedding dress she could have purchased in Fentonville.

Widow Jones baked her delicious cookies for guests and Lula and Jed lent the buggy. Tillie, Mollie, Mrs. Vannostrand, Mrs. Hodgeson, Reverend and Mrs. Harr, and several others donated money to purchase a lovely set of china for Genevieve and Oliver.

Oliver transferred the reins and reached for her hand. "I'm sorry I can't buy you the things Irving could, but you can borrow the Overman safety bicycle anytime you'd like."

There was a glint in his eyes and Genevieve giggled. "It has never mattered to me that you weren't wealthy. And yes, I'd delight in riding the Overman a time or two and perhaps become more proficient at it."

"And I'll bring the swing from the boarding house and hang it here in front of our new house." He pointed at a sturdy tree.

"*Our* new house. I like the sound of that. I'd love for you to move the swing here, Oliver."

Oliver parked the buggy and Genevieve wanted to pinch herself to be sure this dream was real.

"You look beautiful today, Mrs. Bessell."

"You're quite dapper yourself, Mr. Bessell."

He pressed his hand gently into the small of her back as he pulled her closer before capturing her mouth with his. As she reveled in his warm embrace with thoughts of the future on her mind, Genevieve knew her new life with Oliver would certainly be a love most certain.

Do you love books set in historical Montana? Then read on for a sneak peak of *Love in Disguise*, a faith-filled book starring a spunky heroine, a dashing rancher, and bovine-wrought calamity.

READ A SNEAK PEEK FROM

DISGUISE

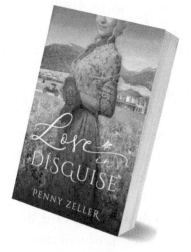

WHO KNEW CONCEALING ONE'S TRUE
IDENTITY COULD BE SO DISASTROUS?

LOVE IN DISGUISE SNEAK PEAK
HOLLOW CREEK, MONTANA, 1911

"THOSE COWS ARE GOING to drive me plumb out of my mind," Emilie Crawford Wheeler muttered. She stood on her porch, hands on her hips, glaring at the herd of Black Angus cows taking a tour of her front yard.

Heart pounding, she reached for the porch pillar for support. Just because she had inherited the ranch from her late husband didn't mean she particularly cared for the abhorrent creatures.

Their boisterous mooing echoed throughout the otherwise quiet Montana afternoon. Emilie watched as they trampled through her yard, destroying or eating every piece of vegetation in their path.

Her beautiful oak tree sapling, which had withstood storms and hail, became the most recent casualty, its tender limbs snapping beneath a particularly large cow's hoof.

One cow swaggered up the porch steps, as if such a feat were an ordinary, everyday spectacle. "Shoo!" she yelled while removing her hat and flapping it about. The cow paid her no mind, but continued to occupy the far end of the porch.

While concentrating on the cow on the porch, Emilie didn't realize until too late that a Black Angus had leaned its head over the railing and commenced chewing on her hat, slowly and methodically, as if it were part of its normal diet. "Well, I never!" she exclaimed.

She best act quickly if she was to halt the destruction of her newly-planted gardens.

Emilie turned on her heel and ran into the house, ignoring the startled looks from her staff. Instead, she reached into the closet and retrieved Newt's shotgun.

"Almira, dear, please do remember proper etiquette and that you must always conduct yourself as a lady." Mother's admonishment using Emilie's given name threatened to stop her from her course of action.

But she must forge ahead on her mission to finally rectify the problem with the neighbor's cows. And why was it the man was never home when she wished to discuss the situation? Did Mr. Evanson even exist? Or did the ranch running parallel to hers operate itself?

Whoever coined the phrase that desperate times called for desperate measures must have dealt with rogue cattle and their propensity to destroy everything in their path.

"Almira, ladies do not fire weapons. Please do reconsider." What Mother might say were she in Hollow Creek thrummed through Emilie's mind.

"Mother, this is an emergency," she said aloud, nearly stomping through the house.

There was no time for proper etiquette. Today Annie Oakley would be her hero. Miss Oakley was a lady, after all, and Emilie thought of just how accurately she might mimic the woman's skill with a gun.

"Is everything all right, Mrs. Wheeler?" Hattie asked, concern lining the maid's youthful features.

"Quite all right, Hattie, thank you for asking."

"Is it the cows again?"

"Yes, it is, and I have every mind to..."

"Will Cook be preparing steak for supper, Emilie?" Vera, her housekeeper, asked as she entered the room, a smirk on her sweet wrinkled face.

Emilie smiled, thankful for the humorous reprieve from the current situation.

Vera placed a hand on Emilie's arm. "Let us help you," she offered. "Morris has gone to town, but surely you, Hattie, and I can do something to deter the cattle until the hands come to rectify the situation. We might be able to save some of your yard."

"Well, someone has to do something about Mr. Evanson's cows." That someone would be her. While it was never admirable to be prone to temper, and Emilie did not consider herself a temperamental woman, she had all she could take with that ninnyhammer Mr. Evanson and his assemblage of bovine.

This was not the first time they demolished her yard, but it would be the last.

"*Almira, do contain yourself,*" Mother would say.

But there was no containing in this matter. Emilie flung open the door and stalked out onto her porch. A few chickens had escaped from the coop and joined the circus in her front yard, squawking and doing their best to avoid being trampled. Emilie checked to be sure no one was in danger of her Annie Oakley ways, then, walking from beneath the porch roof, raised the shotgun to the air and fired a shot.

Several of the cows turned and ran from the yard, but a few stayed staring at her. "Shoo! I said shoo!" Emilie shouted to the remaining cattle.

The cows kicked up dust and continued encroaching upon her property, causing a most appalling commotion.

Jep, one of her hired hands, rounded the corner then, his scrawny torso barely keeping up with his long legs. "We have this all taken care of, Mrs. Wheeler. No need to worry yourself none."

It looked far from taken care of, but Emilie didn't mention such. Two of her other ranch hands appeared on horseback and attempted to herd the cattle back to Mr. Evanson's pasture.

Emilie set the shotgun against the house and patted her skirts, releasing puffs of dust. She was going to faint dead away if she did not get a reprieve from those dastardly cows and their even more dastardly owner.

Vera joined her on the porch. "A trip to Missoula is just the thing you need. Besides, you could deliver those gifts to the orphanage on your way there and see the children."

"What a splendid idea. I shall leave tomorrow morning. However, I think I may just retrieve more presents for the children while in Missoula, and stop there on the way back."

"Excellent plan! Children can never have too many presents. Do you wish for Morris and me to accompany you?"

Emilie thought for a moment, gazing at the seemingly futile effort of Jep and her other hired hands to contain the raucous cattle. "While I do so enjoy the company of you and Morris, I believe I shall make this journey to Missoula on my own."

"Some time away will be of benefit."

Some time away was just what Emilie needed. Being proper-like with a dash of rebellion wasn't for the faint of heart.

Early the following morning, Emilie packed her bags for her trip to Missoula. She needed to retrieve the brand-new hat she'd ordered from Miss Julia Mathilda's Fine Dresses. And not a moment too soon since she was now one hat less due to that cow's insidious appetite. Besides, a break would do her good and shopping did seem to fix many a problem.

Jep carried several wrapped gifts to her Model T to donate to the orphanage. If there was a charity close to her heart, the orphanage would garner that distinction. Each month, she donated a generous check to the institution, as well as a variety of items she purchased in Missoula on her many outings to the city.

Because of the weather and the urgency to return home, she had been unable to stop at the orphanage during her most recent trip. It would be good to stop by, see the children, and gift them with the special books, clothes, and toys she previously purchased for them.

Yes, perhaps a trip to Missoula and the orphanage would improve her mood after having her entire front yard destroyed. At least the west side gardens were unscathed. Huge miracle that was.

Morris started the Model T, opened the door for Emilie to board, and within five minutes, she tasted the freedom of the open road.

Nearly two hours later, she came to a stop at the carriage house behind Missoula's Bellerose Hotel and Restaurant. A fine supper, followed by a restful night's sleep in the feather bed in room twenty-three, the room where she always stayed during her visits, would refresh her mind.

And tomorrow?

Tomorrow the promise of shopping awaited her.

For surely shopping would rid her mind completely of despicable cows and contemptible neighbors.

All would be well.

Oh, why, oh why, had she not chosen to employ the delivery service? No wonder the clerk at Miss Julia Mathilda's Fine Dresses looked askance when she had declined.

Nevertheless, she straightened her posture and attempted to toss aside the twinge of regret. Determination forced her toward her destination and precluded her from turning around and retracing her wobbly steps to Miss Mathilda's.

Emilie stumbled down the boardwalk toward the Bellerose Hotel and Restaurant as she peeked from one side of the tall tower of parcels to the other. They teetered precariously, and with much effort, Emilie righted them. Several folks sauntered past her, most of whom were careful to watch for the woman wearing the oversized wide-brimmed hat with the six boxes and three bags situated in and on her arms.

Where was the Bellerose Hotel and Restaurant? Shouldn't she have reached it by now?

Emilie's right arm had fallen asleep, and her left ached from its awkward position toting the heavy load. Such stubbornness on her part, this endeavor to carry her own parcels.

But was not such an endeavor a necessary part of her newfound freedom? A freedom Emilie had never before experienced? A freedom she planned to embrace?

Pride might be an appropriate term, not that Emilie would admit it.

Mother's choice word for the situation would be *impudent*. She would be shaking her head and her perfectly-coifed curls with dismay at her daughter's choice. Her voice would take on a disapproving tone. *"Almira Emilie Crawford Wheeler,"* she would say, her hands on hips.

Emilie teetered from one foot to the other, desperately trying to balance on the high heels of her fashionable button-up leather boots. The stack of parcels leaned to the left, then to the right. The three bags situated on her arms slid down to her wrists, causing an off-balanced jolt into the stacked parcels.

She was on the verge of recovering from her precarious situation when the most devastating event occurred.

Someone bumped into her right shoulder. It wasn't that it was a hard bump, or even a rowdy bump, but it did totter her nearly plumb off her feet and toward the left.

And her parcel with the new hat? It plummeted to the ground and tumbled into the street. Flinging the rest of her purchases haphazardly to the side, Emilie darted toward the parcel as it rolled into the path of an oncoming wagon. Desperate to save her hat, Emilie absentmindedly stumbled into the path of traffic.

Just as she reached for the prized possession, a strong hand clasped her upper arm and pulled her back onto the boardwalk. Emilie batted at the firm grip, her focus remaining on the parcel.

Her breath squeezed from her lungs, as she watched a horse trample the hatbox and its precious contents. *No. No. No!*

Stunned, Emilie wrenched herself free from the grasp and staggered in shock to retrieve the crushed box. *Surely the hat will be fine. The box is made of only the finest materials.*

She stumbled back to the boardwalk. Holding her breath, she lifted the mangled lid and gaped in horror.

Her precarious situation momentarily forgotten, she winced at the condition of her once-lavish hat. The tattered and formerly ornate ostrich feather floated wistfully to the ground, a sure sign her poor hat had not survived the cruel fate it was handed. Never again would the crushed accessory be wearable.

It had been a splendid hat of 1911 fashion that had boasted a marvelous ostrich feather. Ordered from one of the most renowned millineries in Boston, it emanated elegance and high-class fashion. Now it was ruined.

What was left of it, anyway.

Whatever was she to do? Emilie had intended the new hat to replace the one she wore at present, as the former was becoming far too 1910. While she didn't have too terribly many material weaknesses, she did appreciate the latest fashions.

As if losing a hat to a cow yesterday wasn't bad enough, now she must lose one to a horse.

Could things get any worse? As Emilie lamented her situation, a most ghastly incident occurred. Her toe caught the edge of one of the parcels she had tossed aside, and she lost her footing and tumbled to the ground. She landed in an unladylike heap on the board-walk.

She closed her eyes for a moment, willing that no one saw her unfortunate lack of respectability. *So much for propriety and decorum.*

Then she remembered all of her parcels, especially the once-elegant hat, strewn all about her. Trying not to appear as inept as she felt, Emilie contemplated how best to retrieve those parcels.

And restore her dignity.

A disturbing thought entered her mind: how would she lift the parcels off the ground and re-stack them in her arms?

An even more disturbing thought then clouded her mind.

Would she ever regain her composure?

"Ma'am?"

Emilie gazed up into the bluest of blue eyes she had ever seen. Her eyes locked with his and she sucked in her breath. Suddenly her parcels and her ill-fated hat were forgotten. She squinted at him. His mouth was moving, but in her discombobulated state, she could neither focus on nor hear a word.

In all of her etiquette lessons, never had there been instructions on how to behave properly when sprawled in a most unrefined manner in the middle of the boardwalk in front of a handsome stranger.

Whatever would Mother say now?

If you want to be among the first to hear about the next Ellis Creek installment, sign up for Penny's newsletter through her website. You will receive book and writing updates, encouragement, notification of current give-aways, occasional freebies, and special offers.

AUTHOR'S NOTE

Dear Reader,

I hope you enjoyed reading Genevieve and Oliver's story as much as I enjoyed writing it.

There are always fictional liberties taken when writing a book, and this one is no exception. For those of you who have read the other two books in the series, you'll soon realize that jawbreakers are an ongoing theme. In reality, anyone who ate as many of them as Tillie and Lula (especially Lula) would likely have no teeth and would probably have other health issues as well. But the beauty of writing fiction is that we authors are able to create things that would not otherwise happen in real life. Hence the multiple bags of jawbreakers given to Lula in exchange for her matchmaking expertise.

Researching vintage bicycles was one of many highlights of writing this book. Oliver was the perfect character to own an Overman safety bicycle, and when the idea came to me about nabbing a thief, I couldn't wait to give him an adventure and subsequent hero status.

I would be remiss if I didn't mention a couple of the editing "bloopers" found during the first (of four) rounds of editing. While the most hilarious errors are still when I accidentally typed John Mark from *Dreams of the Heart* going to the salon instead of the saloon (perm, anyone?), and Trey squeezing Carleigh's face instead of her hand in *Love in the Headlines*, there were some laugh-worthy moments in *Love Most Certain*. The most notable were when four lonely words were found all alone in a paragraph—"her oblong face shown". The other was how, by leaving out just one word, it changed the entire meaning of a sentence. Case in point..."I only lived until I was seven." This sentence was removed in its entirety during the third round, but what I meant to write was—"I only lived *there* until I was seven."

Before I was an author, I never realized just how many times a book must be edited before it goes to print or is uploaded as an ebook. Sometimes no matter how many eyes proofread a manuscript, there are still pesky errors that find their way into books. I'm grateful we found the lonely oblong face and the missing word early in the process!

When I first wrote *Love from Afar* for a Barbour Publishing novella collection, I never fathomed return visits to the charming Ellis Creek, Montana. But soon, I realized Tillie's story needed to be written. Before I knew it, Genevieve's story was begging to be next. After all, I missed those lighthearted characters and the excitement of finding new ones to add to the fold.

I've already had readers ask...what about Mollie and Gideon? Will they fall in love? (Or at least admit they are falling in love?) And how will letters be introduced in Book Four?

What about Mr. Norman and Widow Jones? Might they be included in a future book as secondary characters once again? Or Lorelei? Will she move to Ellis Creek and take an interest in working at Tillie's new library?

Lord willing, Mollie and Gid's story will someday come to fruition. The editorial calendar right now is jam-packed with two upcoming new releases in the Wyoming Sunrise Series, as well as, *Over the Horizon*, Book One, in a brand new Christian historical romance series. As such, I can't give you an exact release date for Mollie and Gid. I'm in prayer for God's guidance and timing, and when new details become available, I'll announce them in my newsletter.

Thank you for taking a return visit to the lighthearted and charming town of Ellis Creek!

ACKNOWLEDGMENTS

To my family. As always, thank you for your encouragement and support as I put words to paper.

A special thank you to my oldest daughter for your confidence in me, your willingness to listen to my constant book ideas and offer insight, and your patience in reading over the rough drafts of my scenes, which are never written in order.

To my Penny's Peeps Street Team. Thank you for spreading the word about my books. I appreciate you all so much.

To my readers. May God bless and guide you as you grow in your walk with Him.

And, most importantly, thank you to my Lord and Savior, Jesus Christ. It is my deepest desire to glorify You with my writing and help bring others to a knowledge of Your saving grace.

Let the words of my mouth and the meditation of my heart be acceptable in your sight, O Lord, my rock and my redeemer.
Psalm 19:14

About the Author

Penny Zeller is known for her heartfelt stories of faith and her passion to impact lives for Christ through fiction. While she has had a love for writing since childhood, she began her adult writing career penning articles for national and regional publications on a wide variety of topics. Today, Penny is the author of nearly two dozen books. She is also a homeschool mom and a fitness instructor.

When Penny is not dreaming up new characters, she enjoys spending time with her husband and two daughters, camping, hiking, canoeing, reading, running, cycling, gardening, and playing volleyball.

She is represented by Tamela Hancock Murray of the Steve Laube Agency and loves to hear from her readers at her website www.pennyzeller.com and her blog, *random thoughts from a day in the life of a wife, mom, and author*, at www.pennyzeller.wordpress.com.

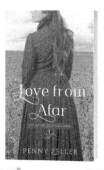

LOVE LETTERS FROM ELLIS CREEK

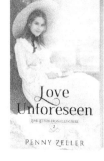

WYOMING SUNRISE SERIES

PURCHASE HERE

— HORIZON SERIES —

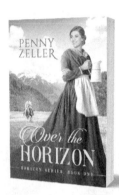

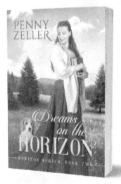

CHRISTIAN
CONTEMPORARY ROMANCE

Love in the Headlines

Chokecherry Heights

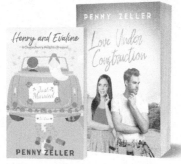

Made in the USA
Las Vegas, NV
09 July 2023

74412901R00105